D0815568

six months,
three days,
five others

TOR BOOKS BY CHARLIE JANE ANDERS

All the Birds in the Sky

Six Months, Three Days, Five Others

six months, three days, five others

charlie jane anders

A TOM DOHERTY ASSOCIATES BOOK

NEW YORK

This is a work of fiction. All of the characters, organizations, and events portrayed in these short stories are either products of the author's imagination or are used fictitiously.

SIX MONTHS, THREE DAYS, FIVE OTHERS

Edited by Patrick Nielsen Hayden

A Tor Book
Published by Tom Doherty Associates
175 Fifth Avenue
New York, NY 10010

www.tor-forge.com

The Library of Congress Cataloging-in-Publication Data
is available upon request.

ISBN 978-0-7653-9489-7 (mini hardcover)

Our books may be purchased in bulk for promotional, educational, or business use. Please contact your local bookseller or the Macmillan Corporate and Premium Sales Department at 1-800-221-7945, extension 5442, or by email at MacmillanSpecialMarkets@macmillan.com.

First Edition: October 2017

Printed in the United States of America

0 9 8 7 6 5 4 3 2 1

To Annalee, with all my heart

contents

six months, three days, five others

The Fermi Paradox Is Our Business Model

The thing about seeking out new civilizations is, every discovery brings a day of vomiting. There's no way to wake from a thousand years of Interdream without all of your stomachs clenching and rejecting, like marrow fists. The worst of it was, Jon always woke up hungry as well as nauseous.

This particular time, Jon started puking before the autosystems had even lifted him out of the Interdream envelope. He fell on his haunches and vomited some more, even as he fought the starving urge to suck in flavors through his feed-holes. He missed Toku, even though he'd seen her minutes ago, subjective time.

Instigator didn't have the decency to let Jon finish puking before it started reporting on the latest discovery. "We have picked up—"

"Just—" Jon heaved again. He looked like a child's flatdoll on the smooth green floor, his body too oval from long recumbence, so that his face grimaced out of his sternum. "Just give me a moment."

Instigator waited exactly one standard moment, then went on. "As I was saying," the computer droned, "we've picked up both radiation traces and Cultural Emissions from the planet."

"So, same as always. A technological civilization, followed by Closure." Jon's out-of-practice speaking tentacles stammered as they slapped together around his feed-holes. His vomit had almost completely disappeared from the floor, thanks to the ship's autoscrubs.

"There's one thing." Instigator's voice warbled, simulating the sound of speaking tentacles knotted in puzzlement. "The Cultural Emissions appear to have continued for some time following the Closure."

"Oh." Jon shivered, in spite of the temperature-regulated, womblike Wake Chamber. "That's not supposed to happen." The entire point of Closure was that nothing happened afterwards. Ever again. At least he was no longer sick to his stomachs (for now anyway) and Instigator responded by pumping more flavors into the chamber's methane/nitrogen mix.

Jon spent two millimoments studying the emissions

from this planet, third in line from a single star. Instigator kept reminding him he'd have to wake Toku, his boss/partner, with a full report. "Yeah, yeah," Jon said. "I know. But it would be nice to know what to tell Toku first. This makes no sense." Plus he wanted to clean up, maybe aim some spritzer at the cilia on his back, before Toku saw him.

At the thought of Toku coming back to life and greeting him, Jon felt a flutter in his deepest stomach. Whenever Jon was apart from Toku, he felt crazy in love with her—and when he was in her presence, she drove him nuts and he just wanted to get away from her. Since they had been sharing a three-room spaceship for a million years, this dynamic tended to play out in real-time.

Jon tried to organize the facts: He and Toku had slept for about two thousand years, longer than usual. Instigator had established that the little planet had experienced a massive radioactive flare, consistent with the people nuking the hell out of themselves. And afterwards, they'd carried on broadcasting electromagnetic representations of mating or choosing a leader.

"This is shit!" Jon smacked his playback globe with one marrow. "The whole point of Closure is it's already over before we even know they existed."

"What are you going to tell Toku?" Instigator asked.

Toku hated when Jon gave her incomplete data. They'd taken turns being in charge of the ship, according to custom, for the first half million years of their mission, until they both agreed that Toku was the better decision maker.

Jon was already fastening the hundreds of strips of fabric that constituted his dress uniform around his arm- and leg-joints. He hated this get-up, but Toku always woke even crankier than he did. His chair melted into the floor and a bed yawned out of the wall so he could stretch himself out.

"I guess I'll tell her what we know, and let her make the call. Most likely, they had a small Closure, kept making Culture, then had a final Closure afterwards. The second one may not have been radioactive. It could have been biological, or climate-based. It doesn't matter. They all end the same way."

At least Jon had the decency to let Toku finish voiding her stomachs and snarling at Instigator's attempts at aromatherapy before he started bombarding her with data. "Hey love," Jon said. "Boy, those two thousand years flew by, huh? The time between new civilizations is getting longer and longer. Makes you wonder if the Great Expedient is almost over."

"Just tell me the score," Toku grumbled.

"Well," Jon said. "We know they were bipedal, like us. They had separate holes for breathing and food consumption, in a big appendage over their bodies. And they had a bunch of languages, which we're still trying to decipher. We've identified manufactured debris orbiting their world, which is always a nice sign. And, uh . . . we think they might have survived."

"What?" Toku jumped to her feet and lurched over, still queasy, to look over Jon's shoulder at his globe. "That doesn't happen."

"That's what I said. So what do we do? The Overnest says not to approach if we think there's a living culture, right? On the other hand, it might be even longer than two millennia before we find the next civilization."

"Let me worry about that," Toku said, sucking in some energizing flavors and slowly straightening up her beautifully round frame. Her speaking tentacles knotted around her feed-holes. "I think we assume they didn't survive. It's like you said: They probably held on for a little while, then finished up."

Space travel being what it was, Jon and Toku had months to debate this conclusion before they reached this planet, which was of course called Earth. (These civilizations almost always called their homeworlds "Earth.") For two of those months, Instigator mistakenly believed that the planet's main language was something called Espanhua, before figuring out those were two different languages: Spanish and Mandarin.

"It all checks out," Toku insisted. "They're ultraviolent, sex-crazed and leader-focused. In other words, the same as all the others. There's absolutely no way."

Jon did not point out that Toku and he had just spent the past two days having sex in his chamber. Maybe that didn't make them sex-crazed, just affectionate.

"I'm telling you, boss," Jon said. "We're seeing culture that references the Closure as a historical event."

"That does not happen." Toku cradled all her marrows.

There was only one way to settle it. Weeks later, they lurched into realspace and settled into orbit around Earth.

"So?" Toku leaned over Jon and breathed down his back, the way he hated. "What have we got?"

"Looking." Jon hunched over the globe. "Tons of lovely metal, some of it even still in orbit. Definitely plenty of radioactivity. You could warm up a lovebarb in seconds." Then he remembered Toku didn't like that kind of language, even during sex, and quickly moved on. "I can see ruined cities down there, and . . . oh."

He double- and triple-checked to make sure he wasn't looking at historical impressions or fever-traces.

"Yeah, there are definitely still electromagnetic impulses," said Jon. "And people. There's one big settlement on that big island. Or small continent." He gestured at a land mass, which was unfortunately lovebarb-shaped and might remind Toku of his dirty talk a moment earlier.

Toku stared as Jon zoomed in the visual. There was one spire, like a giant worship-spike, with millions of lights glowing on it. A single structure holding a city full of people, with a tip that glowed brighter than the rest. These people were as hierarchical as all the others, so the tip was probably where the leader (or leaders) lived.

"Options," Toku said.

Jon almost offered some options, but realized just in time that she wasn't asking him.

"We could leave," Toku said, "and go looking for a different civilization. Which could take thousands of years, with the luck we've had lately. We could sit here and wait for them to die, which might only take a few hundred years. We could go back into Interdream and ask Instigator to wake us when they're all dead."

"It's just so . . . tasty-looking." Jon sighed. "I mean, look at it. It's perfect. Gases, radioactive materials, refined metals, all just sitting there. How dare they still be alive?"

"They're doing it just to mess with you." Toku laughed and Jon felt a shiver of nervous affection in his back-cilia.

She stalked back to her own chamber to think over the options, while Jon watched the realtime transmissions from the planet. He was annoyed to discover the survivors spoke neither Spanish nor Mandarin, but some other language. Instigator worked on a schema, but it could take days.

"Okay," Toku said a few MM later. "We're going back to Interdream, but only level two, so years become moments. And that way, the wake-up won't be too vomit-making. Instigator will bring us out—gently—when they're all dead."

"Sure, boss," Jon said, but then an unpleasant thought hit him. "What if they don't die off? Instigator might let us sleep forever."

"That doesn't hap—" Toku put one marrow over her feed-holes before she jinxed herself. "Sure. Yeah. Let's make sure Instigator wakes us after a thousand years if the bastards haven't snuffed it by then."

"Sure." Jon started refining Instigator's parameters, just to make damned sure they didn't sleep forever. Something blared from the panel next to his globe, and an indicator he'd never seen before glowed. "Uh, that's a weird light. What's that light? Is it a happy light? Please tell me it's happy."

"That's the external contact monitor," Instigator purred. "Someone on the planet's surface is attempting to talk to us. In that language I've been working on deciphering."

It only took Instigator a couple MM to untangle it. "Attention, vessel from [beyond homeworld]. Please identify yourselves. We are [non-aggro] but we can defend ourselves if we need to. We have a [radioactive projectile] aimed at you. We would welcome your [peaceful alliance]. Please respond."

"Can we talk back in their language?" Toku asked.

Instigator churned for a while, then said yes. "Tell them we come from another star, and we are on a survey mission. We are peaceful but have no desire to interact. Make it clear we are leaving soon."

"Leaving?" Jon asked, after Instigator beamed their message down, translated into "English."

"I've had enough of this," Toku breathed. "Not only did they survive their Closure, but they're threatening us with a Closure of our own. Someone else can check on them in a few millennia. Worse comes to worst, we can just overdraw our credit at the Tradestation some more."

"They are launching something," Instigator reported. "Not a projectile. A vessel. It will converge on our position in a few MM."

Watching the blip lift off from the planet's surface, Jon felt a weird sensation, not unlike the mix of hunger and nausea he'd felt when he'd woken from Interdream: curiosity.

"You have to admit, boss, it would be interesting. The first living civilization we've actually met, in a million years of visiting other worlds. Don't you want to know what they're like?"

"I just wish they had the decency to be dead." Toku sighed. "That's by far the best thing about other civilizations: their 100 percent fatality rate."

The little blip got closer, and Toku didn't make any move to take them out of realspace. She must have been experiencing the same pangs of curiosity Jon was. It wasn't as if they'd contacted these people on purpose, so nobody could blame Jon or Toku if they made contact briefly.

Jon reached out with his lower right marrow and grazed Toku's, and she gave him a gentle squeeze.

"What do you want to bet the leader of their civilization is on that ship, engaging in atavistic power displays?" Toku almost giggled. "It would be amusing to see. I mean, we've seen the end result often enough, but . . ."

"Yeah," Jon said. They were each daring the other to be the coward who took the ship out of realspace before that vessel arrived.

The "Earth" ship grazed theirs, trying to do some kind of connective maneuver. Instigator tried a few different things before finally coating the visiting ship's "airlock" with a polymer cocoon. Instigator couldn't make air that the "Earths" could breathe, but could at least provide a temperature-controlled chamber for them in the storage hold.

Three of the "Earths" came into the chamber and figured out a way to sit in the chairs that Instigator provided. In person they looked silly: They had elongated bodies, with "heads" elevated over everything else, as if each person was a miniature hierarchy. "I am Renolz. We are here in [state of non-violence]," the leader of the "Earths" said.

Jon tapped on his communications grid, some sort of all-purpose "nice to meet you" that Instigator could relay to the "Earths."

Slowly, haltingly, the "Earths" conveyed that they were from a city-state called Sidni. And everyone left alive on "Earth" was the servant of someone named "Jondorf" who controlled a profit-making enterprise called "Dorfco." The rest of the "Earths" had died hundreds of years ago, but a few million people had survived inside the "Dorfco" megastructure.

"We always had [optimism/faith] that we weren't alone in the universe," the leader said after a few MM of conversation. "We have waited so long."

"You were never alone," Jon tapped back on his comm-grid. "We made lots of others, just like you, more or less, but you're the first ones we've found alive." He hit "send" before Toku could scream at him to stop.

"What in the slow-rotting third stomach of the Death Lord do you think you're doing?" Toku pushed Jon away from the comm-grid. "You're not supposed to tell them that."

"Oh! Sorry. It just slipped out!" Jon pulled a chair from the floor on the other side of the room from the comm-grid, and settled in to watch from a safe distance.

In reality, Jon had decided to tell the "Earths" the truth because he had that hunger/nausea pang again. He wanted to see how they would react.

"What did you say?" Renolz replied after a moment. "Did you say you made us?"

"No," Toku tapped hastily on the comm-grid. "That was a translation error. We meant to say we found you, not that we made you. Please ignore that last bit. In any case, we will now be leaving your star system forever. Please get off our ship, and we'll be gone before you know it."

"That was no translation error." Renolz looked agitated, from the way he was twitching. "Please. Tell us what you meant."

"Nothing. We meant nothing. Would you please leave our ship now? We're out of here."

"We will not leave until you explain."

"Options," Toku said, and this time Jon knew better than to offer any. She bared her flavor/gas separators at him in anger. "We could expel the 'Earths' into space, but we're not murderers. We could wait them out, but they might launch their projectile and destroy us. We could leave and take them with us, but then they would suffocate. And we're not murderers."

"Why not just explain it to them?" Jon couldn't help asking.

"This is going on your permanent file." Toku's eyes clustered in pure menace. Jon shrank back into the corner.

"Okay then," Toku tapped on the comm-pad. "This may be hard for you to understand, so please listen carefully and don't do that twitching thing again. Yes. We made you, but it's not personal."

"What do you mean, it is not personal?" Renolz seemed to be assuming the most aggressive power stance an "Earth" could take.

"I mean, we didn't intend to create your species in particular. Our employers seeded this galaxy with billions of life-seeding devices. It was just a wealth-creation schema." The worst Interdream nightmare couldn't be worse than this: having to explain yourself to one of your investment organisms. Toku stiffened and flinched, and Instigator pumped soothing flavors into the air in response.

"You mean you created us as a [capital-accretion enterprise]?" The clear bubble on the front of Renolz's helmet turned cloudy, as if he were secreting excess poisonous gases. The other two members of his group kept clutching each other.

"Yeah, that's right," Toku tapped. "We . . ." She wrote, erased, wrote, erased, wrote again. "We created you, along with countless other sentient creatures. The idea is, you evolve. You develop technology. You fight. You dig up all the metals and radioactive elements out of the ground. As you become more advanced, your population gets bigger, and you fight more. When your civilization gets advanced enough, you fight even harder, until you kill each other off. We don't even find out you existed until after you're all dead. That's how it's supposed to work, anyway."

"Why?"

However they had survived their Closure, it obviously wasn't by being superintelligent. Toku mashed her marrows together, trying to think of another way to explain it so Renolz would understand, and then leave them alone. "You dig up the metals, to make things. Right? You find the rare elements. You invent technology. Yes? And then you die, and leave it all behind. For us. We come and take it after you are gone. For profit. Now do you understand?"

"So you created us to die."

"Yes."

"For [industrial exploitation]?"

"That's right. It's cheaper than sending machines to do it. Often, the denser metals and rare elements are hard to reach. It would be a major pain."

Toku hit "send" and then waited. Was there any chance that, having heard the truth, the "Earths" would get back into their little ship and go back home, so Toku and Jon could leave before their careers were any more ruined? With luck, the "Earths" would finish dying off before anyone found out what had happened.

"What kind of [night predators] are you?" Renolz asked.

Toku decided to treat the question as informational. "We are the Falshi. We are from a world 120,000 light years from here. We're bipeds, like you. You are the first living civilization we've encountered in a million years of doing this job. We've never killed or hurt anyone. Now will you leave our ship? Please?"

"This is a lot for us to absorb," Renolz said from the other chamber. "We . . . Does your species have [God/creator beliefs]? Who do you think created your kind?"

"We used to believe in gods," Toku responded. "Not anymore. We're an old enough race that we were able to study the explosion that created the universe. We saw no creator, no sign of any intelligence at the beginning. Just chaos. But we're not your creators in any meaningful way."

Renolz took a long time to reply. "Will you establish trade with us?"

"Trade?" Toku almost laughed as she read it. She turned to Jon. "Do you see what you've done now?"

Anger made her face smooth out, opened her eyes to the fullest, and for a moment she looked the way she did the day Jon had met her for the first time, in the Tradestation's flavor marsh, when she'd asked him if he liked long journeys.

"We trade with each other," Toku tapped out. "We don't trade with you."

"I think I know why we survived," Renolz said. "We developed a form of [wealth-accretion ideology] that was as strong as nationalism or religion. Dorfco was strong enough to protect itself. Jondorf is a [far-seeing leader]. We understand trade. We could trade with you, as equals."

"We don't recognize your authority to trade," Toku tapped. As soon as she hit the "send" area of the comm-pad, she realized that might have been a mistake. Although communicating with these creatures in the first place was already a huge error.

"So you won't trade with us, but you'll sell our artifacts after we die?" Renolz was twitching again.

"Yes," Toku said. "But we won't hurt you. You hurt each other. It's not our fault. It's just the way you are.

Sentient races destroy themselves, it's the way of things. Our race was lucky."

"So was ours," Renolz said. "And we will stay lucky."

Oh dear. Jon could tell Toku was starting to freak out at the way this was going. "Yes, good," she tapped back. "Maybe you'll survive after all. We would be thrilled if that happened. Really. We'll come back in a few thousand years, and see if you're still here."

"Or maybe," Renolz said, "we will come and find you."

Toku stepped away from the comm-grid. "We are in so much trouble," she told Jon. "We might as well not ever go back to Tradestation 237 if anyone finds out what we've done here." Was it childish of Jon to be glad she was saying "we" instead of "you"?

Toku seemed to realize that every exchange was making this conversation more disastrous. She shut off the comm-grid and made a chair near Jon, so she wouldn't feel tempted to try and talk to the "Earths" any more. Renolz kept sending messages, but she didn't answer. Jon kept trying to catch Toku's eyes, but she wouldn't look at him.

"Enough of the silent tactics," Renolz said an hour later. "You made us. You have a responsibility." Toku gave Jon a poisonous look, and Jon covered his eyes.

The "Earths" started running out of air, and decided to go back to their ship. But before they left, Renolz approached the glowing spot that was Instigator's main communications port in that chamber, so his faceplate was huge in their screen. Renolz said, "We are leaving. But you can [have certainty/resolve] that you will be hearing from us again." Instigator dissolved the membrane so the Earth ship could disengage.

"You idiot!" Toku shouted as she watched the ship glide down into the planet's atmosphere. (It was back to "you" instead of "we.") "See what you did? You've given them a reason to keep on surviving!"

"Oh," Jon said. "But no. I mean, even knowing we're out there waiting for them to finish dying . . . it probably won't change their self-destructive tendencies. They're still totally hierarchical, you heard how he talked about that Jondorf character."

Toku had turned her back to Jon, her cilia stiff as twigs.

"Look, I'm sorry," Jon said. "I just, you know, I just acted on impulse." Jon started to babble something else, about exploration and being excited to wake up to a surprise for once, and maybe there was more to life than just tearing through the ruins.

Toku turned back to face Jon, and her eyes were

moist. Her speaking tentacles wound around each other. "It's my fault," she said. "I've been in charge too long. We're supposed to take turns, and I . . . I felt like you weren't a leader. Maybe if you'd been in charge occasionally, you'd be better at deciding stuff. It's like what you said before, about hierarchy. It taints everything." She turned and walked back towards her bedchamber.

"So wait," Jon said. "What are we going to do? Where are we going to go next?"

"Back to the Tradestation." Toku didn't look back at him. "We're dissolving our partnership. And hoping to hell the Tradestation isn't sporting a Dorfco logo when we show up there a few thousand years from now. I'm sorry, Jon."

After that, Toku didn't speak to Jon at all until they were both falling naked into their Interdream envelopes. Jon thought he heard her say that they could maybe try to salvage one or two more dead cultures together before they went back to the Tradestation, just so they didn't have to go home empty.

The envelope swallowed Jon like a predatory flower, and the sickly sweet vapors made him so cold his bones sang. He knew he'd be dreaming about misshapen creatures, dead but still moving, and for a moment he squirmed against the tubes burrowing inside his body. Jon felt lonesome, as if Toku were light-years away instead of in the next room. He was so close to thinking of the perfect thing to say, to make her forgive him. But then he realized that even if he came up with something in his last moment of consciousness, he'd never remember it when he woke. Last-minute amnesia was part of the deal.

As Good As New

Marisol got into an intense relationship with the people on *The Facts of Life*, to the point where Tootie and Mrs. Garrett became her imaginary best friends and she shared every last thought with them. She told Tootie about the rash she got from wearing the same bra every day for two years, and she had a long talk with Mrs. Garrett about her regrets that she hadn't said a proper goodbye to her best friend, Julie, and her on-again/off-again boyfriend, Rod, before they died along with everybody else.

The panic room had pretty much every TV show ever made on its massive hard drive, with multiple backup systems and a fail-proof generator, so there was nothing stopping Marisol from marathoning *The Facts of Life* for sixteen hours a day, starting over again with season one when she got to the end of the bedraggled final season. She also watched *Mad Men* and *The West Wing*. The media server had tons of video of live theater, but Marisol didn't watch that because it made her feel guilty. Not survivor's guilt, failed playwright guilt.

Her last proper conversation with a living human had been an argument with Julie about Marisol's decision to go to medical school instead of trying to write more plays. ("Fuck doctors, man," Julie had spat. "People are going to die no matter what you do. Theater is *important*.") Marisol had hung up on Julie and gone back to the premed books, staring at the exposed musculature and blood vessels as if they were costume designs for a skeleton theater troupe.

The quakes always happened at the worst moment, just when Jo or Blair was about to reveal something heartfelt and serious. The whole panic room would shake, throwing Marisol against the padded walls or ceiling over and over again. A reminder that the rest of the world was probably dead. At first, these quakes were constant, then they happened a few times a day. Then once a day, then a few times a week. Then a few times a month. Marisol knew that once a month or two passed without the world going sideways, she would have to go out and investigate.

She would have to leave her friends at the Eastland School and venture into a bleak world.

Sometimes, Marisol thought she had a duty to stay in the panic room, since she was personally keeping the human race alive. But then she thought: what if there was someone else living, and they needed help? Marisol was premed, she might be able to do something. What if there was a man, and Marisol could help him repopulate the species?

The panic room had nice blue leather walls and a carpeted floor that felt nice to walk on, and enough gourmet frozen dinners to last Marisol a few lifetimes. She only had the pair of shoes she'd brought in there with her, and it would seem weird to wear shoes after two barefoot years. The real world was in here, in the panic room—out there was nothing but an afterimage of a bad trip.

Marisol was an award-winning playwright, but that hadn't saved her from the end of the world. She was taking premed classes and trying to get a scholarship to med school so she could give cancer screenings to poor women in her native Taos, but that didn't save her either. Nor did the fact that she believed in God every other day.

What actually saved Marisol from the end of the

world was the fact that she took a job cleaning Burton Henstridge's mansion to help her through school, and she'd happened to be scrubbing his fancy Japanese toilet when the quakes had started—within easy reach of Burton's state-of-the-art panic room. (She had found the hidden opening mechanism some weeks earlier, while cleaning the porcelain cat figurines.) Burton himself was in Bulgaria scouting a new location for a nanofabrication facility, and had died instantly.

When Marisol let herself think about all the people she could never talk to again, she got so choked up she wanted to punch someone in the eye until they were blinded for life. She experienced grief in the form of freak-outs that left her unable to breathe or think, and then she popped in another *Facts of Life*. As she watched, she chewed her nails until she was in danger of gnawing off her fingertips.

The door to the panic room wouldn't actually open when Marisol finally decided it had been a couple months since the last quake and it was time to go the hell out there. She had to kick the door a few dozen times, until she dislodged enough of the debris blocking it to stagger out into the wasteland. The cold slapped her in the face and extremities, extra bitter after two years at room temperature. Burton's house was gone—the panic room was just a cube half-buried in the ruins, covered in some yellowy insulation that looked like it would burn your fingers.

Everything out there was white, like snow or paper, except powdery and brittle, ashen. She had a Geiger counter from the panic room, which read zero. She couldn't figure out what the hell had happened to the world, for a long time, until it hit her—this was fungus. Some kind of newly made, highly corrosive fungus that had rushed over everything like a tidal wave and consumed every last bit of organic material, then died. It had come in wave after wave, with incredible violence, until it had exhausted the last of its food supply and crushed everything to dust. She gleaned this from the consistency of the crud that had coated every bit of rubble, but also from the putrid sweet-and-sour smell that she could not stop smelling once she noticed it. She kept imagining that she saw the white powder starting to move out of the corner of her eye, advancing toward her, but when she would turn around there was nothing.

"The fungus would have all died out when there was nothing left for it to feed on," Marisol said aloud. "There's no way it could still be active." She tried to pretend some other person, an expert or something, had said that, and thus it was authoritative. The fungus was dead. It couldn't hurt her now.

Because if the fungus wasn't dead, then she was screwed—even if it didn't kill her, it would destroy the panic room and its contents. She hadn't been able to seal it properly behind her without locking herself out.

"Hello?" Marisol kept yelling, out of practice at trying to project her voice. "Anybody there? Anybody?"

She couldn't even make sense of the landscape. It was just blinding white, as far as she could see, with bits of blanched stonework jutting out. No way to discern streets or houses or cars or anything, because it had all been corroded or devoured.

She was about to go back to the panic room and hope it was still untouched, so she could eat another frozen lamb vindaloo and watch season three of *Mad Men*. And then she spotted something, a dot of color, a long way off in the pale ruins.

The bottle was a deep oaky green, like smoked glass, with a cork in it. And it was about twenty yards away, just sitting in one of the endless piles of white debris. Somehow, it had avoided being consumed or rusted or broken in the endless waves of fungal devastation. It looked as though someone had just put it down a second ago—in fact, Marisol's first response was to yell "Hello?" even louder than before.

When there was no answer, she picked up the bottle. In her hands, it felt bumpy, like an embossed label had been worn away, and there didn't seem to be any liquid inside. She couldn't see its contents, if there were any. She removed the cork.

A *whoosh* broke the dead silence. A sparkly mist streamed out of the bottle's narrow mouth—glittering, like the cheap glitter at the Arts and Crafts table at summer camp when Marisol was a little girl, misty like a smoke machine at a cheap nightclub—and it slowly resolved into a shape in front of her. A man, a little taller than she was and much bigger.

Marisol was so startled and grateful at no longer being alone that she almost didn't pause to wonder how this man had appeared out of nowhere, after she opened a bottle. A bottle that had survived when everything else was crushed. Then she did start to wonder, but the only explanations seemed too ludicrous to believe.

"Hello and congratulations," the man said in a pleasant tone. He looked Jewish and wore a cheap suit, in a style that reminded Marisol somewhat of the *Mad Men* episodes she'd just been watching. His dark hair fell onto his high forehead in lank strands, and he had a heavy beard shadow. "Thank you for opening my bottle. I am pleased to offer you three wishes." Then he looked around, and his already dour expression worsened. "Oh, fuck," he said. "Not *again.*"

"Wait," Marisol said. "You're a— You're a genie?"

"I hate that term," the man said. "I prefer wish-facilitator. And for your information, I used to be just a regular person. I was the theater critic at *The New York Times* for six months in 1958, which I still think defines me much more than my current engagement does. But I tried to bamboozle the wrong individual, so I got stuck in a bottle and forced to grant wishes to anyone who opens it."

"You were a theater critic?" Marisol said. "I'm a playwright. I won a contest and had a play produced off-Broadway. Well, actually, I'm a premed student, and I clean houses for money. But in my off-off-hours, I'm a playwright, I guess."

"Oh," the man said. "Well, if you want me to tell you your plays are very good, then that will count as one of your three wishes. And honestly, I don't think you're going to benefit from good publicity very much in the current climate." He gestured around at the bleak white landscape around them. "My name was Richard Wolf, by the way."

"Marisol," she said. "Marisol Guzmán."

"Nice to meet you." He extended his hand, but didn't actually try to shake hers. She wondered if she would go right through him. She was standing in a world of stinky chalk talking to a self-loathing genie. After two years alone in a box, that didn't even seem weird, really.

So this was it. Right? She could fix everything. She could make a wish, and everything would be back the way it was. She could talk to Julie again, and apologize for hanging up on her. She could see Rod, and maybe figure out what they were to each other. She just had to say the words: "I wish." She started to speak, and then something Richard Wolf had said a moment earlier registered in her brain.

"Wait a minute," she said. "What did you mean, 'Not again'?"

"Oh, that." Richard Wolf swatted around his head with big hands, like he was trying to swat nonexistent insects. "I couldn't say. I mean, I can answer any question you want, but that counts as one of your wishes. There are rules."

"Oh," Marisol said. "Well, I don't want to waste a wish on a question. Not when I can figure this out on my own. You said 'not again,' the moment you saw all this. So, this isn't the first time this has happened. Your bottle can probably survive anything. Right? Because it's magic or something."

The dark green bottle still had a heft to it, even after she'd released its contents. She threw it at a nearby rock a few times. Not a scratch.

"So," she said. "The world ends, your bottle doesn't get damaged. If even one person survives, they find your bottle. And the first thing they wish for? Is for the world not to have ended."

Richard Wolf shrugged, but he also sort of nodded at the same time, like he was confirming her hunch. His feet were see-through, she noticed. He was wearing wing tip shoes that looked scuffed to the point of being scarred.

"The first time was in 1962," he said. "The Cuban Missile Crisis, they called it afterwards."

"This is *not* counting as one of my wishes, because I didn't ask a question," Marisol said.

"Fine, fine," Richard Wolf rolled his eyes. "I grew tired of listening to your harangue. When I was reviewing for the *Times,* I always tore into plays that had too many endless speeches. Your plays don't have a lot of monologues, do they? Fucking Brecht made everybody think three-page speeches were clever. Fucking Brecht."

"I didn't go in for too many monologues," Marisol said. "So. Someone finds your bottle, they wish for the apocalypse not to have happened, and then they probably make a second wish, to try and make sure it doesn't happen again. Except here we are, so it obviously didn't work the last time."

"I could not possibly comment," Richard Wolf said. "Although I should say that everyone gets the wrong idea about people in my line of work—meaning wish-facilitators, not theater critics. People had the wrong idea when I was a theater critic, too—they thought it was my job to promote the theater, to put buns in seats, even for terrible plays. That was *not* my job at all."

"The theater has been an endangered species for a long time," Marisol said, not without sympathy. She looked around the pasty-white, yeast-scented death-scape. A world of Wonder Bread. "I mean, I get why people want criticism that is essentially cheerleading, even if that doesn't push anybody to do their best work."

"Well, if you think of theater as some sort of *delicate flower* that needs to be kept protected in some sort of *hothouse*"—and at this point, Wolf was clearly reprising arguments he'd had over and over again when he was alive—"then you're going to end up with something that only the *faithful few* will appreciate, and you'll end up worsening the very marginalization that you're seeking to prevent."

Marisol was being very careful to avoid asking anything resembling a question, because she was probably going to need all three of her wishes. "I would guess that the job of a theater critic is misunderstood in sort of the opposite way than the job of a genie," she said. "Everybody is afraid a theater critic will be too brutally honest. But a genie . . ."

"Everybody thinks I'm out to swindle them!" Richard Wolf threw his hands in the air, thinking of all the *tsuris* he had endured. "When, in fact, it's always the client who can't express a wish in clear and straightforward terms. They always leave out crucial information. I do my best. It's like stage directions without any stage left or stage right. I interpret as best I can."

"Of course you do," Marisol said. This was all starting to creep her out, and her gratitude at having another person to talk to (who wasn't Mrs. Garrett) was getting driven out by her discomfort at standing in the bleached-white ruins of the world kibitzing about theater criticism. She picked up the bottle from where it lay undamaged after hitting the rock, and found the cork.

"Wait a minute," Richard Wolf said. "You don't want to—"

He was sucked back inside the bottle before she finished putting the cork back in.

She reopened the bottle once she was back inside the panic room, with the door sealed from the inside. So nothing or nobody could get in. She watched three episodes of *The Facts of Life*, trying to get her equilibrium back, before she microwaved some sukiyaki and let Richard Wolf out again. He started the spiel about how he had to give her three wishes over again, then stopped and looked around.

"Huh." He sat and sort of floated an inch above the sofa. "Nice digs. Real calfskin on this sofa. Is this like a bunker?"

"I can't answer any of your questions," Marisol said, "or that counts as a wish you owe me."

"Don't be like that." Richard Wolf ruffled his two-tone lapels. "I'm just trying not to create any loopholes, because once there are loopholes it brings everybody grief in the end. Trust me, you wouldn't want the rules to be messy here." He rifled through the media collection until he found a copy of *Cat on a Hot Tin Roof*, which he made a big show of studying until Marisol finally loaded it for him.

"This is better than I'd remembered," Richard Wolf said an hour later.

"Good to know," Marisol said. "I never got around to watching that one."

"I met Tennessee Williams, you know," Richard said. "He wasn't nearly as drunk as you might have thought."

"So here's what I figure. You do your level best to implement the wishes that people give you, to the letter," Marisol said. "So if someone says they want to make sure that a nuclear war never happens again, you do your best to make a nuclear war impossible. And then maybe that change leads to some other catastrophe, and then the next person tries to make some wishes that prevent that thing from happening again. And on, and on. Until this."

"This is actually the longest conversation I've had since I became a wish-facilitator." Richard crossed his leg, ankle over thigh. "Usually, it's just whomp-bomp-a-lula-three-wishes, and I'm back in the bottle. So tell me about your prize-winning play. If you want. I mean, it's up to you."

Marisol told Richard about her play, which seemed like something an acquaintance of hers had written many lifetimes ago. "It was a one-act," she said, "about a man who is trying to break up with his girlfriend, but every time he's about to dump her she does something to remind him why he used to love her. So he hires a male prostitute to seduce her, instead, so she'll cheat on him and he can have a reason to break up with her."

Richard was giving her a blank expression, as though he couldn't trust himself to show a reaction.

"It's a comedy," Marisol explained.

"Sorry," Richard said. "It sounds awful. He hires a male prostitute to sleep with his girlfriend. It sounds . . . I just don't know what to say."

"Well, you were a theater critic in the 1950s, right? I guess it was a different era."

"I don't think that's the problem," Richard said. "It just sounds sort of . . . misanthropic. Or actually woman-hating. With a slight veneer of irony. I don't know. Maybe that's the sort of thing everybody is into these days—or was into, before the world ended yet again. This is something like the fifth or sixth time the world has ended. I am losing count, to be quite honest."

Marisol was put out that this fossil was casting aspersions on her play—her *contest-winning play,* in fact. But the longer she kept him talking, the more clues he dropped without costing her any wishes. So she bit her lip.

"So. There were half a dozen apocalypses," Marisol said. "And I guess each of them was caused by people trying to prevent the last one from happening again, by making wishes. So that white stuff out there. Some kind of bioengineered corrosive fungus, I thought—but maybe it was created to prevent some kind of climate-related disaster. It does seem awfully reflective of sunlight."

"Oh, yes, it reflects sunlight just wonderfully," Richard said. "The temperature of the planet is going to be dropping a lot in the next decade. No danger of global warming now."

"Ha," Marisol said. "And you claim you're just doing the most straightforward job possible. You're addicted to irony. You sat through too many Brecht plays, even though you claim to hate him. You probably loved Beckett as well."

"All right-thinking people love Beckett," said Richard. "So you had some *small* success as a playwright, and yet you're studying to be a doctor. Or you were, before this unfortunate business. Why not stick with the theater?"

"Is that a question?" Marisol said. Richard started to backpedal, but then she answered him anyway.

"I wanted to help people, really help people. Live theater reaches fewer and fewer people all the time, especially brand-new plays by brand-new playwrights. It's getting to be like poetry—nobody reads poetry any more. And meanwhile, poor people are dying of preventable cancers every day, back home in Taos. I couldn't fool myself that writing a play that twenty people saw would do as much good as screening a hundred people for cervical cancer."

Richard paused and looked her over. "You're a good person," he said. "I almost never get picked up by anyone who's actually not a terrible human being."

"It's all relative. My protagonist who hires a male prostitute to seduce his girlfriend considers himself a good person, too."

"Does it work? The male prostitute thing? Does she sleep with him?"

"Are you asking me a question?"

Wolf shrugged and rolled his eyes in that operatic way he did, which he'd probably practiced in the mirror. "I will owe you an extra wish. Sure. Why not. Does it work, with the gigolo?"

Marisol had to search her memory for a second, she had written that play in such a different frame of mind. "No. The boyfriend keeps feeding the male prostitute lines to seduce his girlfriend via a Bluetooth earpiece—it's meant to be a postmodern Cyrano de Bergerac—and she figures it out and starts using the male prostitute to screw with her boyfriend. In the end, the boyfriend and the male prostitute get together because the boyfriend and the male prostitute have seduced each other while flirting with the girlfriend."

Richard cringed on top of the sofa with his face in his insubstantial hands. "That's terrible," he said. "I can't believe I gave you an extra wish just to find that out."

"Wow, thanks. I can see why people hated you when you were a theater critic."

"Sorry! I mean, maybe it was better on the stage. I bet you have a flair for dialogue. It just sounds so . . . hackneyed. I mean, *postmodern Cyrano de Bergerac*? I heard all about postmodernism from this one graduate student who opened my bottle in the early 1990s, and it sounded dreadful. If I wasn't already sort of dead, I would be slitting my wrists. You really did make a wise choice, becoming a doctor."

"Screw you." Marisol decided to raid the relatively tiny liquor cabinet in the panic room, and poured herself a generous vodka. "You're the one who's been living in a bottle. So. All of this is your fault." She waved her hand, indicating the devastation outside the panic room. "You caused it all, with some excessively ironic wish-granting."

"That's a very skewed construction of events. If the white sludge *was* caused by a wish that somebody made—and I'm not saying it was—then it's not my fault. It's the fault of the wisher."

"Okay," Marisol said. Richard drew to attention, thinking she was finally ready to make her first wish. Instead, she said, "I need to think," and put the cork back in the bottle.

Marisol watched a season and a half of *I Dream of Jeannie*, which did not help at all. She ate some delicious beef stroganoff and drank more vodka. She slept and watched TV and slept and drank coffee and ate an omelet. She had no circadian rhythm to speak of anymore.

She had four wishes, and the overwhelming likelihood was that she would foul them up, and maybe next time there wouldn't be one person left alive to find the bottle and fix her mistake.

This was pretty much exactly like trying to cure a patient, Marisol realized. You give someone a medicine which fixes their disease but causes deadly side effects. Or reduces the patient's resistance to other infections. You didn't just want to get rid of one pathogen, you wanted to help the patient reach homeostasis again. Except that the world was an infinitely more complex system than a single human being. And then again, making a big wish was like writing a play, with the entire human race as players. Bleh.

She could wish that the bioengineered fungus had never dissolved the world, but then she would be faced with whatever climate disaster the fungus had prevented. She could make a blanket wish that the world would be safe from global disasters for the next thousand years—and maybe unleash a millennium of stagnation. Or worse, depending on the slippery definition of "safe."

She guessed that wishing for a thousand wishes wouldn't work—in fact, that kind of shenanigans might be how Richard Wolf wound up where he was now.

The media server in the panic room had a bazillion movies and TV episodes about the monkey paw, the wishing ring, the magic fountain, the Faustian bargain, the djinn, the vengeance-demon, and so on. So she had plenty of time to soak up the accumulated wisdom of the human race on the topic of making wishes, which amounted to a pile of clichés. Maybe she would have done more good as a playwright than as a doctor, after all—clichés were like plaque in the arteries of the imagination, they clogged the sense of what was possible. Maybe if enough people had worked to demolish clichés, the world wouldn't have ended.

Marisol and Richard sat and watched *The Facts of Life* together. Richard kept complaining and saying things like, "This is worse than being trapped inside a bottle." But he also seemed to enjoy complaining about it.

"This show kept me marginally sane when I was the only person on Earth," Marisol said. "I still can't wrap my mind around what happened to the human race. So, you *are* conscious of the passage of time when you're inside the bottle." She was very careful to avoid phrasing anything as a question.

"It's very strange," Richard said. "When I'm in the bottle, it's like I'm in a sensory deprivation tank, except not particularly warm. I float, with no sense of who or where I am, but meanwhile another part of me is getting flashes of awareness of the world. But I can't control them. I might be hyperaware of one ant carrying a single crumb up a stem of grass, for an eternity, or I might just have a vague sense of clouds over the ocean, or some old woman's aches and pains. It's like hyper-lucid dreaming, sort of."

"Shush," said Marisol. "This is the good part—Jo

is about to lay some Brooklyn wisdom on these spoiled rich girls."

The episode ended, and another episode started right away. You take the good, you take the bad. Richard groaned loudly. "So what's your plan, if I may ask? You're just going to sit here and watch television for another few years?" He snorted.

"I have no reason to hurry," Marisol said. "I can spend a decade coming up with the perfect wishes. I have tons of frozen dinners."

At last, she took pity on Richard and found a stash of PBS *American Playhouse* episodes on the media server, plus other random theater stuff. Richard really liked Caryl Churchill, but didn't care for Alan Ayckbourn. He hated Wendy Wasserstein. Eventually, she put him back in his bottle again.

Marisol started writing down possible draft wishes in one of the three blank journals that she'd found in a drawer. (Burton had probably expected to record his thoughts, if any, for posterity.) And then she started writing a brand-new play, instead. The first time she'd even tried, in a few years.

Her play was about a man—her protagonists were always men—who moves to the big city to become a librarian, and winds up working for a strange old lady, tending her collection of dried-out leaves from every kind of tree in the world. Pedro is so shy, he can't even speak to more than two people, but so beautiful that everybody wants him to be a fashion model. He pays an optometrist to put drops in his eyes, so he won't see the people photographing and lighting him when he models. She had no clue how this play was going to end, but she felt a responsibility to finish it. That's what Mrs. Garrett would expect.

She was still stung by the idea that her prize-winning play was dumb, or worse yet kind of misogynistic. She wished she had an actual copy of that play, so she could show it to Richard and he would realize her true genius. But she didn't wish that out loud, of course. And maybe this was the kick in the ass she needed to write a better play. A play that made sense of some of this mess.

"I've figured it out," she told Richard the next time she opened his bottle. "I've figured out what happened those other times. Someone finds your bottle after the apocalypse, and they get three wishes. So the first wish is to bring the world back and reverse the destruction. The second wish is to make sure it doesn't happen again. But then they still have one wish left. And that's the one where they do something stupid and selfish, like wishing for irresistible sex appeal."

"Or perfect hair," said Richard Wolf, doing his patented eye-roll and air-swat.

"Or unlimited wealth. Or fame."

"Or everlasting youth and beauty. Or the perfect lasagna recipe."

"They probably figured they deserved it," Marisol stared at the pages of scribbles in her hands. One set of diagrams mapping out her new, as-yet-unnamed play. A second set of diagrams trying to plan out the wish-making process, act by act. Her own scent clung to every surface in the panic room, the recirculated and purified air smelled like the inside of her own mouth. "I mean, they saved the world, right? So they've earned fame or sex or parties. Except I bet that's where it all goes wrong."

"That's an interesting theory," said Wolf, arms folded and head tilted to one side, like he was physically restraining himself from expressing an opinion.

Marisol threw out almost every part of her new play, except the part about her main character needing to be temporarily vision-impaired so he can model. That part seemed to speak to her, once she cleared away the clutter about the old woman and the leaves and stuff. Pedro stands, nearly nude, in a room full of people doing makeup and lighting and photography and catering and they're all blurs to him. And he falls in love with one woman, but he only knows her voice, not her face. And he's afraid to ruin it by learning her name or seeing what she looks like.

By now, Marisol had confused the two processes in her mind. She kept thinking she would know what to wish for, as soon as she finished writing her play. She labored over the first scene for a week before she had the nerve to show it to Richard, and he kept narrowing his eyes and breathing loudly through his nose as he read it. But then he said it was actually a promising start, actually not terrible at all.

The mystery woman phones Pedro up, and he recognizes her voice instantly. So now he has her phone number, and he agonizes about calling her. What's he afraid of, anyway? He decides his biggest fear is that he'll go out on a date with the woman, and people will stare at the two of them. If the woman is as beautiful as Pedro, they'll stare because it's two beautiful people together. If she's plain-looking, they'll stare because they'll wonder what he sees in her. When Pedro eats out alone, he has a way of shrinking in on himself, so nobody notices him. But he can't do that on a date.

At last, Pedro calls her and they talk for hours. On

stage, she is partially hidden from the audience, so they, too, can't see what the woman looks like.

"It's a theme in your work, hmmm?" Richard Wolf sniffed. "The hidden person, the flirting through a veil. The self-loathing narcissistic love affair."

"I guess so," Marisol said. "I'm interested in people who are seen, and people who see, and the female gaze, and whatever."

She finished the play, and then it occurred to her that if she made a wish that none of this stuff had happened, her new play could be unwritten as a result. When the time came to make her wishes, she rolled up the notebook and tucked it into her waistband of her sweatpants, hoping against hope that anything on her immediate person would be preserved when the world was rewritten.

In the end Pedro agrees to meet the woman, Susanna, for a drink. But he gets some of the eye-dilating drops from his optometrist friend. He can't decide whether to put the drops in his eyes before the date—he's in the men's room at the bar where they're meeting, with the bottle in his hand, dithering—and then someone disturbs him and he accidentally drops the bottle in the toilet. And Susanna turns out to be pretty, not like a model but more distinctive. She has a memorable face, full of life. She laughs a lot, Pedro stops feeling shy around her. And Pedro discovers that if he looks into Susanna's eyes when he's doing his seminude modeling, he no longer needs the eye drops to shut out the rest of the world.

"It's a corny ending," Marisol admitted. "But I like it."

Richard Wolf shrugged. "Anything is better than unearned ambivalence." Marisol decided that was a good review, coming from him.

Here's what Marisol wished:

1) I wish this apocalypse and all previous apocalypses had never happened, and that all previous wishes relating to the apocalypse had never been wished.
2) I wish that there was a slight alteration in the laws of probability as relating to apocalyptic scenarios, so that if, for example, an event threatening the survival of the human race has a ten percent chance of happening, that ten percent chance just never comes up, and yet this does not change anything else in the material world.
3) I wish that I, and my designated heirs, will keep possession of this bottle, and will receive ample

warning before any apocalyptic scenario comes up, so that we will have a chance to make the final wish.

She had all three wishes written neatly on a sheet of paper torn out of the notebook, and Richard Wolf scrutinized it a couple times, scratching his ear. "That's it?" he said at last. "You do realize that I can make anything real. Right? You could create a world of giant snails and tiny people. You could make *The Facts of Life* the most popular TV show in the world for the next thousand years—which would, incidentally, ensure the survival of the human race, since there would have to be somebody to keep watching *The Facts of Life*. You could do anything."

Marisol shook her head. "The only way to make sure we don't end up back here again is to keep it simple." And then, before she lost her nerve, she picked up the sheet of paper where she'd written down her three wishes, and she read them aloud.

Everything went cheaply glittery around Marisol, and the panic room reshaped into The Infinite Ristretto, a trendy café that just happened to be roughly the same size and shape as the panic room. The blue-leather walls turned to brown brick, with brass fixtures and posters for the legendary all-nude productions of Mamet's *Oleanna* and Marsha Norman's *'night, Mother.*

All around Marisol, friends whose names she'd forgotten were hunched over their laptops, publicly toiling over their confrontational one-woman shows and chamber pieces. Her best friend, Julia, was in the middle of yelling at her, freckles almost washed out by her reddening face.

"Fuck doctors," Julia was shouting, loud enough to disrupt the whole room. "Theater is a direct intervention. It's like a cultural ambulance. Actors are like paramedics. Playwrights are *surgeons,* man."

Marisol was still wearing Burton's stained business shirt and sweatpants, but somehow she'd gotten a pair of flip-flops. The green bottle sat on the rickety white table nearby. Queen was playing on the stereo, and the scent of overpriced coffee was like the armpit of God.

Julia's harangue choked off in the middle, because Marisol was giving her the biggest stage hug in the universe, crying into Julia's green-streaked hair and thanking all her stars that they were here together. By now, everyone was staring at them, but Marisol didn't care. Something fluttery and heavy fell out of the waistband of her sweatpants. A notebook.

"I have something amazing to tell you, Jools," Marisol breathed in Julia's ear. She wanted to ask if Obama was still president and the Cold War was still over and stuff, but she would find out soon enough and this was more important. "Jools, I wrote a new play. It's all done. And it's going to change *everything.*" Hyperbole was how Marisol and Julia and all their friends communicated. "Do you want to read it?"

"Are you seriously high?" Julia pulled away, then saw the notebook on the floor between their feet. Curiosity took over, and she picked it up and started to read.

Marisol borrowed five bucks and got herself a pour-over while Julia sat, knees in her face, reading the play. Every few minutes, Julia glanced up and said, "Well, okay," in a grudging tone, as if Marisol might not be past saving after all.

Intestate

1. road trip

The minivan is already full of children when it pulls up to my front steps. I climb into the deepest pit facing out the back door, and plunk my rucksack in my lap. Before I even buckle up, my youngest niece, Rosemary, is grabbing at my jeans leg and trying to show me a doll, while her brother Sebastian is threatening to shoot me with a toy gun. The whole van smells like mildew and overripe fruit. Empty juice boxes scatter over my feet. This will be a long ride.

"Welcome aboard, Emmy. Next stop, Castle von Doom," my youngest brother, Eric, says from the front seat. His brown hair is receding, and he's grown a wispy soul patch. Next to him, his latest wife, Octavia, is trying to find indy folk-rock on the iPod. They both wave at me, and then we're off. Eric drives faster than you would think a man driving a vanload of his own children would go, even on the back roads full of hairpin turns and big trees.

Eric keeps joking about how we're going to visit Doctor Doom, his newest nickname for our father. "He's going to bake us doomcookies," Eric says.

"Doomcookies!" Rosemary shouts.

"Made with doomberries," Octavia says.

"Doomberries!" we all shout, even me. I only feel a little disloyal to my father.

The hills are full of disappearing acts, like sheep meadows and barns that pop out for just a few moments. There's almost too much color to take in, between the trees that are going red and swaths of evergreens. Rosemary asks if she can count the sheep, or if that will make her doze off. I tell her to try, and see what happens. We are driving in the middle of the road, directly over the yellow lines, when a jeep comes around the tight bend and nearly rams into us. Eric swerves back into our lane, hyperventilating a little. Next to me, Rosemary has fallen asleep.

We get lost twice, and have to stop for pee breaks and ice cream and hot dogs, but we're still the first to arrive at the failed gated community where my dad lives. We roll off the main road into a small feeder road, which leads to a broken gate, and then a cul-de-sac with five driveways. The last one goes to a big McMansion with two gables and a huge lawn in front, and acres of forest in back. The other four driveways lead to dirt lots or to empty, collapsing houses. As we roll up the rocky driveway on grumbling tires, my dad skips out the front door. His white beard and glasses catch the sunlight. Even though it feels like the day has gone on forever, it's only noon.

"It's Doctor Doom," Eric says with no sarcasm.

2. my father's hands

When I was little, my father was a pair of hands. Later, he was a torso that I fell into like sleep. Maybe, occasionally, he was rough laughter just over my head.

The first time I could remember being aware of my father as a whole person was when he changed. He went away on a research trip, and when he came home, he'd grown a beard and gotten a pair of thick glasses. All of a sudden, this stranger was kissing my mother and moving around us kids as though he had a right. He smelled yeasty. I hadn't been conscious of what my dad looked like before, but this was clearly some kind of home invader, who had tricked everybody. I ran and hid under my mom's dresser.

Now, my father's hands move almost too fast for me to make out clearly. He carves a honey-baked ham to make sandwiches for us, and he flips the carving knife around like a Benihana chef while the kids cheer. Nobody knows exactly what he's done to upgrade his hands, under all the liver spots and calluses. We know better than to ask.

"Don't teach the kids to play with knives, Dad," Eric says at last.

Two nights ago, my sister, Joanna, called me, the first time we'd talked in months. "You know you're probably going to get the hands, Emmy," she said randomly at one point. "You're his favorite, even after everything. You could probably get whichever parts of him you wanted." Joanna is the only one of us kids who inherited Dad's genius; she got a math Ph.D. and even helped solve some theorems and things. She wound up being a super-actuary at one of the top insurance companies, and she can rattle off the chances of anything bad happening to anyone.

My father picks up Rosemary and Sebastian in

each arm, holding them up to his Santa beard and cradling them. He bounces on the balls of his feet like he's about to start Lindy-hopping.

I turn away for a second, and see a strange tapestry on the sitting room wall, way on the other side of the house. And then I realize, it's not a tapestry. It's a beehive in a glass case, open to a small apiary out back.

My dad comes up behind me, almost soundless, and touches my bare shoulder. His fingers are cool and a little sandpapery. "Looking good, Em. You've cut your hair in a bob, and gotten yourself a pair of glasses with baroque frames," he says, by way of saying, "I see you." He seems distracted. For a moment his hand stays in place and we watch the bees together, and I wonder if this means that we've patched things up between us. Or if we're just pretending we've patched it up, and if there's any difference. I try not to wonder if this is one of our last real moments together.

"Happy eightieth birthday, Dad," Eric says, joining us, lite beer in hand. "I hope I look half as good when I'm your age."

3. intellectual property

By late afternoon Friday, pretty much everyone has arrived, and my dad's house, the embarrassingly named Thimblewick, is overrun. There are my three older brothers and one older sister, plus their fourteen children and even a few grandchildren. There are only two bedrooms inside the house, besides my dad's, and by common consent those go to the families with babies: My nephew Derek and his twin daughters Marjorie and Isabella, and my nephew Roger and his son, Gregor.

And yes, Isabella's last name is Pinch, like almost all of us. We all call her Izzy, though "Izzy Pinch" is still kind of ludicrous. She'll just have to own it, I guess.

The rest of us wind up putting up tents, all over the lawn and the clearing out back before the woods. Dad swears the bees are practically wintering already, and won't bother us. Of course, everybody starts getting stung, until Dad closes some vent. We build three bonfires, including one on the front lawn, where we dig a huge pit. It hardly matters—one of the banks will take the house soon enough.

After dark, Dad produces two turkeys and a bloated turducken from a massive oven, and starts carving them on a big folding table in the backyard. He can carve two turkeys simultaneously, although after he notices people watching he starts focusing on just one at a time. He shifts his weight effortlessly as he moves around the table. My sister, Joanna, is watching carefully, to see how he does it. Joanna's hair has gone mostly gray, and she's gotten hatchet-faced.

Joanna told me she expects to inherit Dad's pelvis and hips, when he dies. She thinks he developed some sort of technology that would revolutionize hip replacements everywhere. A new self-lubricating type of acetabular, plus there's a gel in his hip sockets that's full of these special bacteria that Dad found in the Antarctic that absorb the impact when his feet strike the ground, and turn it into energy.

It's undeniably creepy the way Joanna covets her father's pelvis.

Someone has set up speakers in the backyard, playing classic Motown and Stax. The music doesn't even begin to drown out the lamentation of the children, who have just realized that (a) they're camping out in the cold, (b) there's only enough hot water for a few showers at any given time of day, and (c) there's no internet or cell-phone service. I hear one of my nieces, Deedee I think, explaining very seriously that if she can't get online for two days, she will have lost all social status. Forever.

"I figure we've got a day, tops, until it's full-on *Hunger Games* out here," Eric says, like he relishes the idea.

All of the adults stay up late, drinking pungent scotch and reminiscing around the biggest bonfire. At least some of the kids get their usual bedtimes revoked as well, so that there are little white blobs running around us and shrieking. Every few minutes a kid comes running up and says that a kid hit another kid, and someone has to do something.

I wind up sitting next to my father, close enough to the fire that my face and eyes get dehydrated and I'm flushed, and it is like a perfect facsimile of emotional openness. My father sits perfectly straight, his spine effortlessly creating the posture of an eighteen-year-old Alexander technique student. His neck is a very pale green.

"I'm surprised," I say, "you can sit this close to the fire. Don't you have some parts that'll melt or something?"

My dad just laughs and cocks his head.

With the loose clothes my father is wearing, you can't even tell what he's replaced. Most of the legs, for sure. The hip joints. The spine. The skin on his neck, of course. Rumor has it that his whole rib cage is some kind of hydrogen-based generator now. My dad can drink whiskey and eat spicy food without being in horrible pain afterwards, because he's upgraded his stomach and turned his appendix into some kind of backup filtration unit. He can breathe smoky air better than I can. Nobody will know for sure what he's done until someone cuts him up.

Neither of us has talked in a while. I get the feeling my dad is trying to say something that I need to hear. I try to make a silence that he can speak into. We both stare straight ahead, at the pillar of fire. Eventually, my middle brother Dudley comes up and says that there's a problem with the toilets. Both of them. My dad laughs and says he'll get his plumbing tools. I stay by the fire, hoping eventually I'll feel sleepy.

My father told me a hundred stories that he made up on the spot when he used to tuck me in at night, but I forgot them all and he claims he did too. Intellectual property is like that, he told me once. You can write ideas down but then they get trapped in a shape they can't grow out of. That wasn't the reason he'd started confining his biomechanical innovations to just his own body, though—it was more because his body was the one thing his creditors couldn't ever take away. He was in debt so deep, he had to become a limited liability corporation and then sue himself out of existence.

4. two boats

Saturday morning, my dad announces he's taking a hike in the woods. Anyone who wants to is welcome to join him. He also claims the woods are deer tick–free, although he won't say why. He passes out identical bright red scarves for everybody, so that we all look like carolers. Or cultists.

Everybody's so bored by this point that we all agree to go along with him, although that means that our departure gets endlessly delayed because somebody's baby needs to be changed, or there would be hell to pay if my nephew Stephen doesn't have a juicebox.

"I've been trying to keep my kids from going off in the woods by themselves," my brother Dudley says. "Even though when we were kids, we ran around in the woods all the time. Now, though, I keep thinking there could be snakes or raccoons. Raccoons can be vicious. I don't want my kids getting the idea it's okay to wander." Dudley has gained a lot of weight lately, and it suits him.

"I thought the reason people kept their kids on a leash nowadays was because they were worried about kidnappers and pedophiles," I said. "And you know, there's probably none of those within a hundred miles of here. We could look it up, do a Megan's Law thing, if we had the internet."

I might be infertile. I might not. My ex and I tried for a few years, with no luck. But I never wanted to go get the tests because if they found something, then it would be a medical problem all of a sudden, and I'd be trapped on the conveyer belt. My dad taught me early on that sometimes the secret to happiness is figuring out which questions you're better off not answering.

My oldest brother, Robert, thinks my father experimented on me in the womb and that's why I can't have children. But Robert would be ready to believe almost any horror story about Dad.

Finally, we're all ready to go on the hike, and then somebody realizes that one of the children is a fake. That is, he's not any of our kids. He doesn't even look like a member of our family. He's too perfect, too blond and towheaded. Everybody always checks to make sure their own kids are all accounted for, but nobody ever checks to see if there are too many children. My brother Robert and I drag the kid, whose name is Nicky, inside the house to interrogate him, and it only takes a few minutes before he confesses: he's an infiltrator. Nicky's a child actor, whose main claim to fame is being a featured extra during the third season of *He's The Champ*, and his talent agency has repurposed him for corporate espionage. He won't say who his client is, it could be any of a dozen companies.

"I'll drive him to the nearest town and drop him off," Robert says.

"I'll ride with you," I say. So the two of us get in Robert's hatchback and drive to Somerset in total silence, with Nicky in the backseat staring at us. We leave Nicky at a Friendly's with a pay phone, and we give him five bucks.

There's no kid listening in on our conversation on the way back, but Robert and I still don't talk to each other. Robert's almost old enough to be my father himself, but he looks much older than that.

When Robert is parking, on the side of the driveway near the bottom, I ask him what part of Dad he thinks he'll inherit.

Robert pauses in the middle of pulling up the parking brake. He looks at me for the first time. "The feet," he says at last. "You notice Dad is never barefoot, and he wears those clown shoes. I think he's got transgenic monkey feet, or something along those lines. He never loses his balance." Then he gets out of the car and jogs up to the house, where everybody is ready to walk into the woods.

Joanna was the one who spread this idea that we would each get a piece of Dad when he passed away. She had some phone conversation with him where he said we would all be provided for, and we would all have something to remember him by. She swears he was pretty explicit about the arrangement.

My father is much taller than I remember, taller even than he was yesterday. His grandchildren cluster around his waist, asking him questions about himself. At first I think they're actually curious about Grandpa's wartime experiences in Korea, like when he got kidnapped by pirates from Pusan who were raiding Taiwanese shipping in an old gunboat, and he drank too much homemade *soju* and saw some sort of "maenad" floating over the sea foam. But no. The kids are just trying to get my dad to explain how to get the internet turned on.

None of us brought a cell phone, so we have no

way of keeping track of time, but it feels like an hour later when we finally come through the woods into a big clearing. A boat looms out of the tall grass and blanched dandelions. It's an old-fashioned sailing ship, and you can glimpse a big wooden steering wheel on deck. It's wooden, and half rotted, but the seven sails are clean and crisp and white.

Rosemary squeals and runs towards the boat, but my dad grabs her and scoops her up, putting a finger to his lips.

A deer comes out of the wide-open side of the boat, then looks at us. No horns, but a huge sinewy body, as tall as I am. A doe, then. Her body is dotted with clouds. She stands for a moment, then scampers into the forest. Another deer comes out of the boat, then another and another.

"It's the deer boat," my father says. As if he's just proved something to us, that he's been claiming all along.

5. metal birds

Several years ago, my father stopped talking to me. He didn't announce he was cutting me off, and I didn't notice for a few weeks, or maybe even longer.

And then I thought it was just another one of those queasy Dad moments, like when I converted to Christianity, or when I came out as a lesbian. It took a while to know for sure: this was different. My father was making a point of not talking to me, even when I spoke directly to him, like at a family dinner or something.

My mom was still alive, and I pleaded with her to tell me what was going on, but she said she didn't feel like playing telephone with my dad and me. Mom was tired a lot. Nobody thought it meant anything.

I went home and stalked my dad. He still walked with a limp from his Korean War injury back then, so he couldn't get away from me. "Please," I said, "please just tell me. Whatever it is we'll fix it. There can't be something so bad we can't make it right, between us, you can build anything, and I make problems go away for a living. Please, Dad. Dad. This could be the last time we see each other, are you really going to waste it shutting me out? Please just say something." He just gazed at me like there were no words. His neck gave off a pale green bioluminescence, because it was dusk.

Weeks passed, maybe months. I was bucking for a promotion at Real Outcome Solutions, so I only thought about my dad's latest weirdness every now and then. And then my mom was officially sick and that took precedence.

One day my father sent me an email, with just a link to a video, about a minute long. A drone aircraft, a UAV, was flying over the desert, more graceful than any airplane with people inside could ever be. The plane coasted and then dove, like it was going to buzz someone's house in the wilderness. And then a streak of smoke came out of it, and the house burst. The next thing you saw was a crater.

The videos started coming every few days after that, beautiful instructional films and blurry cell-phone footage, always showing metal birds in the desert.

After a few weeks, my father sent a link to an article about how my company had helped secure the government contract for these UAVs with a particular contractor. I remembered sitting in on some of those meetings, but it wasn't my baby or anything. And another article about civilian deaths. And a few days later, a third article, about how that company was suing my father and some of his friends over patents.

I never knew which pissed my father off more: that his designs were helping to kill babies, or that he was getting ripped off.

My mom's survival chances dropped below 40

percent and we gave up on the radiation and the cyberknife. I took indefinite leave and moved back home to help take care of Mom. Eventually, Dad and I had to start talking again, because it's hard to avoid speaking to someone when you're each supporting one arm of a dying person.

6. the announcement

Saturday night, someone has rigged up a tire swing on a branch, which breaks and nearly kills Deedee. We need one car to go pick up groceries, and a separate van for the booze run. Everybody is looking at the tent city surrounding the house and making loud, meaningful groans. The bonfires are twice as big as the night before.

"It's like a medieval siege." Eric gestures at the tents ringing my dad's fake castle. "It just needs a moat and some catapults. I'm kind of surprised my dad doesn't have an alligator moat, actually."

"Shark moat," Octavia says. "Not alligator moat. A mad scientist always has a shark moat."

"After this, we've done our duty, for like ever," Dudley's wife, Ayanna, is saying on the other side of the big fire. "This is the big reunion, and after this we're golden for like a year or two. Right?"

"I sure freaking hope so," Dudley says under his breath, but still kind of loud. Dudley grew up thinking he would always be the youngest sibling, until eventually Eric and I were born and he was just another middle kid.

"This is probably Dad's last chance to torture all of us at the same time." Robert has come up beside Dudley, Ayanna and me, hot dog in one hand and red plastic cup in the other. "Efficiency has always been a paramount value to him."

A while later, Joanna claims that my father offered to make a batch of LSD for any of his grandchildren who wanted some, as long as they were over the age of fifteen.

"Is it true?" I ask my dad in the backyard, where he's toasting marshmallows. "Did you really offer to make acid for your grandkids? Who are running around, in proximity to three large open flames?"

My dad just shrugs and says that at his age, the best you can hope for is to have good stories told about you. Then he's swallowed by darkness.

By midnight, there is a nearly constant howling coming from all around us. Living in a city, you forget how dark the world can get. I feel like if I quit drinking vodka, I will start feeling prematurely hungover. I have had too much chocolate. Every few minutes, a child runs over my legs. I am remembering that I promised to help out with child care this weekend, as the only childless adult here. The damp, freezing walk to the house for a bathroom break and vodka nearly breaks me.

"'Will' is a weird word," says Eric, who used to be a novelist and also a teacher, among many other things. "I mean, it's the most future-looking word in the English language. We talk about what 'will' happen. But when you actually *will* something to happen, we use the word 'shall,' not 'will.' And we reserve the verb 'will' for things that are going to happen, whether you will them to or not. And when someone dies, their final message to the future is their will and testament. Testament, of course, being a word that only has to do with the past, because you testify about what's already happened. So 'will and testament' is like the future and the past in one document, except that it's just a pointless list of material objects."

We've all been avoiding mentioning the question of dad's will, at least overtly, but Eric is an asshole. Eric already mentioned that he wants dad's spine, he thinks it has some kind of carbon fiber nanotube thing.

The sun comes up, with its usual memory-erasing properties. The moment sunlight hits my retinas, the previous seven hours become an indistinct dream. My father and I are the last two people standing, near the ugly smouldering pit in the front yard. I am wearing two coats, and still feel colder than I can ever remember feeling. Dad's glasses are misted up. He does tai chi.

"Happy birthday," I tell him.

There's another big silence, and then I try to tell Dad that I'm sorry about the UAV thing. I know it was wrong. And as far as I'm concerned, he and I are good. I hope he thinks we're good too. Whatever happens going forward, I hope we've found forgiveness for each other. And so on.

He puts his left hand on my shoulder. "We're family, Em," he says in my ear. Is it my imagination, or is there a clickety-clack vibration coming from his palm? "We never forgive each other. That's what separates families from just any random assortment of people."

Then he walks away, faster than I could hope to keep pace with, because he has a thousand waffles worth of batter to pour.

I sit down on the very edge of the pit and stare into the ashes. The ground is dew-soaked. The tents start jostling as people wake up from almost no sleep. The grown-ups cry out for coffee, the children start asking how soon they can go home. Eric is convinced he's lost one of his children, until we find her sleeping in the linen closet. I keep staring ahead and downward. My eyes are full of floaters.

"Hey," says my teenage nephew Terence. "They told me to come tell you that there are waffles. Plus Grandpa Mervyn has an announcement or something."

We all crowd inside the kitchen/living room, two dozen of us perched on whatever furniture didn't go in the bonfire. My father stands at a table piled with waffles, pinging a mimosa glass with a tea spoon. "If I could have your attention," he says.

Joanna nudges me, like *this is it*. Robert and I catch each other's eye for a second, and he shrugs with his hands up. Eric leans forward in his chair, nearly knocking Sebastian and Rosemary off his lap.

My father pauses, milking the suspense. He sips his mimosa and says, "I'm sorry to have to tell you all, I have cancer. It's already metastasized. I waited too long to get rid of the other lung. Stupid mistake. Most of you will probably never see me alive after today." He starts passing out waffles, asking people if they want a pat of butter on top, so that nobody has a chance to ask him any questions.

Halfway through the waffle breakfast, we notice that my father has vanished. The metal door leading to his basement laboratory is locked. And there's a laminated sign saying not to enter, because the air down there is not breathable to normal humans. I make a halfhearted attempt to pound on the door. Joanna tries to talk Dad out of there, but he doesn't talk back.

An hour later, I'm back in the minivan. Eric is driving twice as fast as before, on almost no sleep. As we crest a giant hill and a dozen windmills appear, Eric says randomly, "I guess we'll have to wait to find out who gets which part of Dad until we hear the reading of the will. I'm kind of glad nobody gets to call dibs on anything." I get a spasm in my shoulder from twisting around to see where we're going, so I give up and settle for a view of the lengthening road behind us.

My father has never told us much about the weird vision he saw as a young man at sea, except that he called it a maenad and it seemed holy. Although he mentioned once, when I got my first training bra, that the maenad had a dozen breasts, each shaped like a perfect tidal wave. The maenad rose out of the sea spray, almost translucent, and its gaze seemed to encompass the whole of the rusty gunship before narrowing down to my father. The maenad appeared to smile at Dad. That's how he knew it was time to go home.

The Cartography of Sudden Death

Ythna came to the Beldame's household when she was barely old enough to walk. They took her from the nursery block in the middle of the night, with nothing but the simple koton robe she was wearing, and carried the tiny girl to a black shiny vehicle, a Monopod. Sitting in the back, wearing a neat gray uniform and matching black gloves and shoes, was an Officiator, who asked the young Ythna some questions. The next thing she knew, she was riding a white cage on a wire over the mountains, up to the gilded fortress where she would serve the Beldame for the rest of her days, if she was lucky.

Ythna forgot the Officiator's face, or whatever else he said to her, but she would always remember what he said as she stepped, barefoot, out of the cage as the sun rose over the golden house. He knelt before her and spoke gently: "You are but one of a thousand retainers to the Beldame. But each of you is a finger, or a toe. Your movements are her movements. Do not make her a disgrace."

Ythna lived in a tiny yellow dormitory room with nine other small children, all of them sharing white-and-red uniforms and eating from the same dispensary. Ythna learned to read and write basic Gaven texts, and worked in the cavernous kitchen and boiler room of the golden fortress, which was called Parathall. At night, the other children teased Ythna and pinched her in places where the bruises wouldn't show on her golden-brown skin, under her retainer uniform. Two girls, the pale, blonde Maryn and the olive-toned Yuli, appointed themselves the rulers of Children's Wing, and if Ythna didn't please Maryn and Yuli she found herself sealed inside a small wooden linen box, suffocating, sometimes overnight.

Every moment people weren't looking, Ythna wept into her loose sleeve. Until one day when she brought some hot barley wine to the Beldame herself, doing the five-point turn as she'd been taught, ending up on one knee with the tray raised before the wrought-iron chair.

Ythna was eight or nine years old, and she made

sure not to look at the Beldame's white round face, as she knelt. But in Ythna's eagerness to avoid looking on her mistress, she found herself gazing, instead, at the papers the Beldame was studying. Ythna started reading them, until the Beldame noticed.

"You can read that?" the Beldame said.

Ythna nodded, terrified.

"And tell me, what do you think of it?" the Beldame asked.

Ythna stammered at first, but at last she shared a few thoughts about the document, which dealt with the rebellious offworld colonists, and the problems with maintaining order in the fringes of the Empire here on Earth. The Beldame asked more questions, and Ythna answered as best she could. After that, the Beldame sent her away—but then Ythna found herself chosen to bring food and drink to the Beldame often. And sometimes, the Beldame would invite her to sit for a moment at her feet, and talk to her.

Years passed. One day, word came that the Beldame was going to be elevated to the Emperor's Thousand, so she would be in the same direct relationship to the Emperor that the Beldame's thousand retainers were to her. There would be a massive ceremony at the Tomb of the Unknown Emperor, at which the Beldame would be given a steel thimble, symbolizing the fact that she was becoming one of the Emperor's own fingers. Ythna couldn't even imagine that she could be one-thousandth of the woman who was one-thousandth of the Emperor. She watched the sunrise between the mountain peaks below the Beldame's arched picture windows and laughed at the floor brush in her hand.

"A lot is going to change for all of us," said Maryn, who had grown into a striking young woman who still bossed around the other retainers. "Strange foods, new places. All the more reason to keep our behavior perfect. The Beldame is counting on us."

Ythna said nothing. She was still smaller than Maryn, barely noticeable except for her ribbons of long black hair, down to her waist, and the way she ran through the stone passages of the fortress, her bare feet as silent as snow melting, when nobody else was around.

The day came nearer, and they all traveled for a week by steam truck and Monopod to the Tomb of the Unknown Emperor. At last, they saw it in the distance, looming over the plains: a great structure, shaped like an old letter M, with two great pillars supporting the black canopy. The Unknown Emperor had lain in state for over a hundred years there, behind a faceless statue that raised one hand to the people who'd served him without knowing his name.

They all lined up in rows, the thousand of them, at the base of the Tomb, while the Beldame climbed to the very top. Some of the retainers were playing small bells, and sweet smoke was coming up out of brass pipes all around them. The Officiators were leading Ythna and the others in ceremonial chants. Ythna could see the tiny figure of the Beldame, emerging on top of the structure, as the Emperor himself bestowed the thimble on her. A voice, one of the Chief Officiators, spoke of the hundreds of years of tradition they honored today.

Ythna thought that she could not be any more deliriously proud than she was at this moment, watching her friend and mistress elevated. Her only wish was that she could see the Beldame Thakrra up close at this moment, to behold the look on Thakrra's face.

A second later, Ythna had her desire. The Beldame lay on the ground directly in front of her, lying on her back, her small body broken by the fall from the top of the structure. Her gentle, lined face was still recognizable, inside her brocaded robe and twelve-peaked silken hat, but she had no expression at all, and blood was leaking out all over the ground, until it lapped against Ythna's bare feet. She could not help but panic that maybe her selfish wish had caused this to happen.

Next to Ythna, Maryn saw the Beldame's corpse and began wailing in a loud, theatrical fashion. The other retainers heard Maryn and followed her lead, making a sound like a family of cats. Ythna, meanwhile, could barely choke out a single tear, and it hurt like a splinter coming out.

Frantic to avoid seeing the Beldame like this, Ythna looked up—just as a strange woman stepped out of the nearest pillar in the Tomb. The woman had long curly red hair under a pillbox hat shaped like one of the lacquered discs where the Beldame had kept her spare monocles. She had a sharp nose and chin, and quick gray eyes. And she wore a long black coat, with embroidered sleeves and shoulders, and shiny brass buttons with cords looping around them. She looked like a commanding general from an old-fashioned foreign army.

The red-haired woman stepped forward, looked around, and took in the scene. Then she said a curse word in a language that Ythna had never heard, and slipped away around the side of the Tomb, before anybody else noticed her.

Hours went by. Ythna felt as though her rib cage were as barbed and twisted as the ends of the Beldame's beloved wrought-iron chair. She knelt on the ground, in the Beldame's dried blood, weeping, though the Beldame's body was long gone. Nearby, Yuli and Maryn were making a huge show of singing the Bottomless Grief Spiral chant along with the Officiators. But Maryn kept whispering to Yuli that maybe they should make a break for it—retainers whose mistress died could not count on being given new positions elsewhere, and the alternative was Obsolescence.

"We can't escape," Yuli whispered back. "Not with everybody watching. And where would we go? There is no place to hide in the entire Empire, from sea to pole to sea."

Ythna couldn't stop wondering about the red-haired woman, who wore no uniform Ythna recognized, and who had all but spat on the ground on seeing the gathered retainers and Officiators. She finally crept over to the pillar she'd seen the woman step out of, and started feeling around for a hinge or join, some evidence of a passageway. The Tomb had many hidden ways in and out—that was how the Emperor's body had been deposited there without anyone seeing his face—but if there was a doorway here, then Ythna could not find it. She tried to shake the granite edge of the pillar with her fingertips, as if she could bring down the mighty Tomb by herself.

"What do you think you are doing?"

Ythna turned to see one of the Obfuscators watching her. Trex. He'd arrived with the others, to take charge of the scene and keep the retainers in order. He was a tall, solidly built man with a sallow face and black hair and eyes. And he was holding a fully charged valence gun, aimed at her. She could smell the burnt-shoe odor from a few feet away, and if he fired she would be a pile of dust in seconds. He had the black chestpiece and square helmet that indicated he was one of the Emperor's personal Obfuscators, empowered to create order in just about any way he deemed necessary.

Ythna backed against the pillar, stuttering and trying to think of what to say. "There was a woman, a stranger. Not one of our party. She came out of this pillar right after the Beldame was killed." She described the woman and her clothing as best she could, and the Obfuscator Trex seemed to be listening carefully. At last, he nodded and indicated for her to rejoin the others.

"Tell nobody else what you saw," added Trex. Then he stalked away, his back and legs as stiff as one of the supply robots carrying fuel and food up the mountainside to the Golden Fortress.

The retainers all started to freeze as the sun got lower on the horizon, since they were wearing light koton ceremonial gowns designed for comfort in the noon sun. The patch of dried blood had gone crisp, but the smell of newly slaughtered cattle still hung in the air. Nobody had yet decided what to do with these surplus retainers. Yuli and Maryn still debated running away.

Someone gave the retainers hot barley wine, to warm them up, which just reminded Ythna of the Beldame Thakrra all over again, and she found herself crying harder than ever as she drank from the communal jug. Some time later, she needed to relieve herself, and couldn't bear to soil the same ground where the Beldame had bled to death. She begged an Obfuscator until he gave her permission to go around the Tomb to the front entrance, where some simple latrines had been set up. Ythna thanked him profusely.

The latrines were lined up like sentry boxes,

perpendicular to the front pillar of the Tomb. Beyond them, there was the edge of a dense forest of oaks, birches, and pines, stretching all the way to the distant white mountains. A chill wind seemed to come from the woods as Ythna slipped inside one of the latrines, hiking up her shift. When she came out again, the red-haired woman was there.

The woman gestured for Ythna to be silent. "I've been observing you," she whispered, with an accent that Ythna couldn't place. "You're cleverer than the rest. And you're actually grief-stricken for the poor dead Beldame. All your friends are just pretending. I want to help you."

"You killed her," Ythna said. "You killed the Beldame. I saw you step out of the tomb right after she fell."

"No, I swear I had nothing to do with her death," the woman said sadly. "Except that it created a door for me to step through. That's how I travel. My name is Jemima Brookwater, and I'm from the future."

Ythna studied the strange red-haired woman for a moment. Her black boots were shiny but scuffed, her puffy pants had a grass stain on one knee, and her fine velvet coat had a rip in the side, which had been hastily sewn and patched. Whatever this woman was—crackwit, breakbond, or something else—she was not an assassin. But maybe Ythna should tell Trex in any case.

"It was good to meet you, Jemima," Ythna said. "I should go and rejoin the others. Be safe." She turned to go back around the tomb toward the other retainers, whom she could hear chanting the grief spiral with dry, exhausted throats.

"Let me help you," Jemima said again.

Ythna turned back. "Why would you want to help me?"

"I told you, I travel by using the openings created when someone important dies unexpectedly. And I feel bad about that. So I made a vow: every time I travel, I try to help one person, one deserving person."

"And how would you help me?" Something about this woman's way of speaking reminded Ythna of the Beldame, except that Jemima was more animated and lacked the Beldame's dignity.

"I don't know. You tell me. It's not really helping if I decide for myself what sort of help you need, is it?"

Ythna didn't say anything for a moment, so Jemima added:, "Tell me. Your mistress, Thakrra, is dead. What do you want to do now?"

Nobody had ever asked Ythna what she wanted, in

her entire life. But more startling than that was to hear Jemima say Thakrra was dead, by name, because it hit her all over again: the feeling of hopelessness. Like she had swallowed something enormous, that she could never digest even if she lived forever. She heard the droning chant from the plains on the other side of the tomb, and all of a sudden the voices sounded genuinely miserable instead of forced and dried out.

"There is nothing you can do for me," Ythna said, and turned to leave in the shadow of the great criss-crossing limbs of the Tomb.

The woman chased after her, speaking quickly. "That's just not true," she said. "I really don't want to tell you what you should do, but I can help with anything you choose. For example, I can get you out of here. That forest is full of landmines, but I know a secret underground passage, which archaeologists discovered hundreds of years from now. And I could forge whatever documents you might need. Your Empire outlawed proper computers. They keep obsessive records on paper, but with a few major flaws. You can be anyone."

Ythna turned back one last time, tears all over her face. "I cannot be anyone," she said. "I can only be what I am: one small piece of the Beldame. Who do you belong to? Are you completely alone? You seem like someone who just comes and goes, like a ghost. And you want me to become a ghost as well. I can't. Leave me alone."

"Listen." Jemima grabbed Ythna's arm. They were almost back within view of the massed group of retainers, Obfuscators, and Officiators. "This is not going to go well for you. I've read the history books, I know what happened to a retainer whose master or mistress died suddenly, without making arrangements first. If you're lucky, you get reeducated and sent to a new household, where you'll be the lowest status and they'll treat you like dirt. If you're unlucky . . ."

Ythna tried to explain, with eyes full of tears and a voice suddenly hoarse from crying and chanting, that she didn't care what happened to her. "I can't just dishonor the Beldame by running away. That would be worse than enduring any abuse. If you know so much, then you have to understand that."

At last, Jemima let go of Ythna's arm, and she turned to go back to the others before she was missed.

"At least I tried," Jemima said. "I do admire your conviction."

"There she is," a voice said from behind them. "I told you. I told you she was conspiring. All along, conspiring. And scheming." Maryn stood at the edge of the tomb, pointing at Ythna and Jemima. Beside her, Obfuscator Trex advanced, raising the brass rod of his valence gun. Maryn was a foot shorter than Trex and wore simple robes like Ythna's next to Trex's bulky chrome-and-leather uniform. But Maryn's excitement and triumph made her seem twice as big as the strong, fussy man.

Jemima grabbed Ythna and pushed her behind herself, so that Jemima could take the brunt of Trex's first shot and Ythna would have an extra few seconds to live.

"The penalty for conspiring to assassinate a Beldame is death," Trex said, chewing each syllable like a nugget of fat. "I am mightily empowered to carry out the sentence at once."

"I don't want any reward," Maryn said. Everybody ignored her.

"Wait," Jemima said. "You are being duped here. I know you're an intelligent man, I've read about you. Trex, right? I know all about your illustrious career. And I have a perfectly sensible explanation for everything you've witnessed." Jemima was reaching into a tiny holster hidden in the braided piping on the side of her velvet coat, reaching for an object the size of her thumb. A gun.

"Please," Ythna said to Trex. "We didn't conspire. I only just met this woman."

But Trex aimed his valence gun, sparks coming from the connecting tubes, and said, "You are both found guilty, and your sentence is—"

Ythna closed her eyes, waiting for a sizzling noise and the acrid stench of Jemima being torn molecule from molecule. Instead, she heard Maryn scream and thrash the air. When Ythna opened her eyes, Trex's headless body was falling to the ground, and Trex's head was rolling to a stop at Maryn's feet, an expression of supreme disgruntlement forever sealed on Trex's face.

A man wearing a black uniform, as simple as Trex's was ornate, was running away, sheathing a bloody sword of a curved design that Ythna had never seen before. An opaque helmet, shaped like a teardrop, obscured the man's features.

Jemima gave another one of her foreign cursewords and ran after the man. Ythna took one look at the headless Obfuscator and the wailing Maryn—whose screams were likely to bring everybody running—and followed Jemima.

The man with the sword reached the outermost pillar of the M-shaped tomb, and ran through the wall without breaking stride. One moment he was there, the next he was gone. Jemima and Ythna reached the wall a moment later, and Jemima ran straight for the spot where the man had vanished. And then she, too, was gone. Ythna's momentum carried her forward before she could even think about the insanity of what she was doing. She hit the massive-blocked granite wall at the same point as the other two, and felt a sensation like a million tiny hands tugging at her. And then her senses were stolen away, one by one. But not before she had a glimpse of a million bright threads of different colors, crisscrossing around her in the midst of infinite darkness.

Ythna foundered, unable to see, hear, or touch anything for an age, until those same tiny hands grabbed her and shoved her forward, into the light.

For a moment, Ythna was dazzled and had pins and needles in her hands and feet, then she slowly regained her sight. She was lying on the floor of a long high-vaulted chamber, open to the air on one side and closed off on the other. A giant terrace, or balcony, then. The walls to her left were incredibly ornate, with what looked like molded silver encrusted with countless priceless jewels—and yet, someone had gone to great trouble to make that opulence look as ugly as possible. The silver was smudgy gray, the rubies and diamonds were as dull as you could make them. To Ythna's left, past the railing, she could see an endless phalanx of people in retainer outfits, not all that different from what she wore every day, marching forward to the grim, repetitive droning of horns.

Next to Ythna, Jemima was on her knees, covering her face with one hand, and saying, "No, no, no, no, please no," over and over again.

"What is it?" Ythna said. "What's wrong?" She put one hand on Jemima's epauletted shoulder.

"This is the worst place," Jemima said, uncovering her face and gesturing past the balcony at the thousands of people walking in neat rows. "I'm sorry. This is my fault. I shouldn't have brought you here. I wanted to help you, and I've just made everything worse."

"What place? Where are we?" Ythna was still having a hard time thinking straight after the disorientation of passing through the senseless tangle of threads.

"Roughly seventy years after your time. The Glorious Restoration. The worst period in the history of the Gaven Empire." Jemima straightened up a bit on her haunches. "An attempt to restore traditional values to an empire that had grown decadent. They've probably executed another Chief Officiator, and that's what made the door we just came out of. And those people down there? They're marching to the death camps."

"*We're in the future,*" Ythna said, and now she was pulling her own hair to try and get her head straight.

The whole thing sounded mad. But they weren't at the Tomb of the Unknown Emperor any more, and the more she looked at the scene outside, the more she noticed little incongruities.

Like, the retainers marching forward across the square wore simpler uniforms than she'd ever seen before, with a different insignia. The banners hanging on the outer wall of the courtyard, opposite the balcony, listed a different Imperial Era: the Great Rejoicing Era, not the Bountiful Era that Ythna was used to. So there was a different Emperor on the throne. But the banners looked old. And the Obfuscators herding these retainers across the courtyard wore helmets with weird spikes on them, and their chestpieces were a blockier design as well, aimed at protecting against a different class of weapons. Their valence guns were much smaller and could be carried with one hand, too. There were other details, but those were the ones that jumped out at Ythna.

"How did we get here?" Ythna said.

"I told you," Jemima said. "That's how I travel. But I've never killed anyone to open a portal. Trex was supposed to live another few decades, and become the Chief Obfuscator to the Emperor Maarthyon. And I'm sorry, but Beldame Thakrra always died on that day. Her death is in my history book, and I'm pretty sure it was an accident."

Jemima was searching the terrace for clues to the exact date, while trying to stay out of sight from the people below, or on the other balconies further along. "If we know what day this is, then we can know when the next significant death will be," Jemima said. "We need to get the blazes out of here."

"And any death of an important person will make a door?" Ythna said.

"It must be an unexpected death," Jemima said. "Something that creates a lot of causal torsions." Ythna must have looked confused, because she added: "A lot of adjustments. Like ripples."

"So you really are a ghost," Ythna said. "You belong to no one, you travel through death, and you come and go without being seen. I feel sorry for you."

Jemima didn't have anything to say that For the second time in half an hour she had lost her unflappable good humor. She stared at Ythna for a moment.

Then she turned and pointed with one slender gloved finger. "Over there. He's making for that dais. We must stop him, or he'll ruin absolutely everything."

The man with the opaque tear-shaped helmet had his sword out again, with traces of Trex's blood still on it. He was running along another terrace, just around a corner of the giant building from the one where Jemima and Ythna stood. And when Ythna leaned dangerously out into the open, over the stone railing, she could see the man's destination: a dais facing the courtyard, where a bald, sweaty man sat watching the thousands of people being herded away to the slaughter. The man's robes, dais, and throne were like the walls of this chamber: ornate, but ugly and drained of color. Everything about him was designed to show off wealth, without sharing beauty.

At least twenty Obfuscators and Officiators stood between the man with the sword and the man on the throne, who had to be a Vice Emperor. They all aimed their valence guns at the assassin, who raised a long metal brace strapped to his left forearm, which he held in front of him like a shield. The valence guns made the scorching sound Ythna had heard before, but without effect. The man's forearm glowed with a blue light that spread in front of him and seemed to protect him. He reached the first of the Obfuscators, and put his sword through her stomach in an elegant motion that did not slow his run at all.

"How is he doing that?" Ythna said. "With the valence guns?"

Then she turned and realized Jemima wasn't next to her any more. She was already at the far end of the terrace, opening a hidden door she'd found, which led to the next terrace along. Jemima was rushing toward the assassin and the Vice Emperor. Ythna did her best imitation of Jemima's strange foreign swear word—"fth'nak"—and ran after her.

In the next terrace, a group of Officiators were holding up ceremonial trowels, symbolizing the burial of the past and the building of the future, and they gasped when two strange women came running into the space, a tall redhead in a fancy coat and a small dark girl in old-fashioned retainer clothes.

"The Vice Emperor," Jemima gasped without slowing her run. "I'm the only one who can save him."

For a moment, Ythna thought the Officiators might believe Jemima and let her pass. But they fell back on an Officiator's ingrained distrust of anyone or anything that didn't instantly fit, and reached out to try and restrain both Ythna and Jemima. They were too slow—Jemima had almost reached the far wall, and Ythna was slippery as a wet goose—but they called for Obfuscators to help them. By the time Ythna reached the far wall, where Jemima was trying to open the next door, people were firing valence guns at her from the courtyard below. The balcony next to them exploded into chunks of silver and bejeweled masonry.

"Don't worry," Jemima said. "They mass-produced those guns cheaply in this era. At this range, they couldn't hit a Monopod."

She got the door to the next terrace open, and they were facing three Obfuscators aiming valence guns. At point-blank range.

"Guh," Jemima said. "Listen. That reprehensible man over there is about to assassinate your Vice Emperor." By now they were close enough to have an excellent view, as the last few of the Vice Emperor's Obfuscators fought hand-to-hand against the sword-wielding assassin, surrounded by the fresh corpses of their brethren. "I can stop him. I swear to you I can."

These Obfuscators hesitated—long enough for Jemima to pull out the thumb-sized gun hidden in her coat's braid and shoot them all with it. There was a bright pink flash in front of each of them, just before they all fell facedown on the ground.

"Stunned," she said. "They'll be fine."

Then she lifted one arm, so that a bit of lace cuff flopped out of her velvet sleeve, and aimed at the top of the ceremonial gate between the courtyard and the Vice Emperor's dais. A tiny hook shot out of her lace cuff, with a steel cord attached to it, and it latched on to the apex of the gate's arch, right on top of the symbol for Dja-Thun, or the unbroken chain of thousands from Emperor to gutterslave. "Hang on tight," Jemima said, right before she grabbed Ythna's waist and pressed a button, sending them sailing through the smoky bright air over the men shooting valence guns at them. The sun lit up Ythna's face in mid-swing, the same way it once had from the Beldame's window.

By the time they reached the dais, dismounting with only a slight stumble, the assassin had killed the last Obfuscator, and was advancing on the Vice Emperor, who cowered on his massive gray-gold throne.

"Listen to me," Jemima shouted at the man. "You don't want to do this. You really, really do not. Time-travel via murder is a dead end. Literally. You'll tear the map apart, and none of the major deaths of history will happen on schedule. You'll be every bit as lost as I will."

The man turned to salute Jemima. "Professor Brookwater," he said in a low voice, only slightly muffled by his milky helmet. "You are one of my all-time heroes. But you don't know the full potential of what you discovered. I sincerely hope you do get home someday."

Jemima shot at him and missed. He spun, low to the ground, and then pivoted and took the Vice Emperor's head clean off. Almost at once, Ythna could see an indistinct doorway appear on the elaborately carved side of the gray dais: like a pinwheel with too many spokes to count, opening outwards and showing a secret pathway through death and time. Somehow, Ythna couldn't see these doors until she had already passed through one.

The assassin ran into the pinwheel and vanished. The remaining Obfuscators and retainers were crying out from the courtyard below, and a hundred valence guns went off all at once. The dais was collapsing into rubble. Ythna was paralyzed for a moment, until Jemima grabbed her and threw her into the doorway the assassin had created.

The next thing Ythna knew, she landed facedown on a hard cement surface, outdoors, under a nearly cloudless sky. In front of her was a big chain-link fence, with men in unfamiliar uniforms walking past it holding big bulky metal guns. She heard a voice saying indistinct words over a loudspeaker. She turned and saw a row of giant rocket ships looming in the distance, with a flaming circle painted on each gunmetal shell and a mesh of bright scaffolding clinging to their sides.

She couldn't see the assassin with the sword, but Jemima was crouched next to her, looking pissed off and maybe a little weepy.

"It just gets better and better," Jemima said. "This is—"

"I know where we are, this time," Ythna said. "The Beldame showed me pictures. This was the last great assault on the Martian Colony. The Emperor Dickon's great and glorious campaign to bring the principle of Dja-Thun to the unruly people on Mars. This happened decades before I was born."

"It's happening right now," Jemima said, looking in all directions for the man they'd been chasing. "I wonder who just died here."

"What did you mean, about the map?" Ythna said. "You said he was tearing the map apart."

"I've got a history book," Jemima said without pausing her search. "I know the major deaths, down to the exact place and time. Every time I travel,

I chart where each death leads. I'm deciphering the map slowly, but this cad will render that impossible. I've done twenty-eight trips so far, including today."

"How many people have you helped?" Ythna said. "Twenty-seven?"

"Twenty-five," Jemima said.

"And how did that turn out for them?"

"No idea. People like you don't get mentioned in the history books, even if I found an updated version. No offense. But if I ever get home, I can try to look up some detailed records, and try to find out what happened to all of you."

Jemima cursed again in her own language: "Fth'nak." An old-fashioned wheeled vehicle was rolling toward them, with figures in bulky black armor holding big oily guns. The jeep rumbled, a cloud of dust in its wake, as it grew bigger until it was right in front of them. On the side of the jeep was the round, fiery insignia of the Age of Advancement, the Emperor Dickon's era. The men in the front of the truck wore the same image on their helmets.

Jemima started to try and explain their presence to these men, but they cut her off.

"Desertion is a capital crime, as you are no doubt aware," the man in the truck's passenger seat said.

"But you're lucky. The *Dauntless* is short-crewed and ammunition is precious. So I'm going to pretend you didn't just try to run away. That's a one-time offer, good only if you come with me right now. Your new home lifts off tomorrow morning at oh-five hundred hours."

And that's how Jemima and Ythna found themselves in a bare gray cage with a tiny window that gave them a partial view of the nearest rocket, a snub-nosed, squat monstrosity with nine thrusters arrayed like petals. Ythna rubbed the bruises she'd gotten from the guards' rifle butts and rough hands.

"At least they don't think we're spies," said Ythna. "Or they'd have just executed us."

"They assume that nobody could ever get this far inside their security perimeter undetected," said Jemima. "So they reached for the next logical explanation: we must be members of the galley crew, who tried to make a break for it. Instead of executing us, they'll just send us up in one of those ships, probably in irons in case we actually are saboteurs."

"The Beldame told me that this campaign was a terrible waste. The whole assault force died without ever reaching Mars, because the colonists had superior weapons. They used technology that the Empire had rejected as impure," said Ythna. "It was one of the Beldame's lessons that she liked to tell: A just cause becomes unjust when it costs too much human life."

"The Beldame sounds like she was a wise woman," said Jemima.

Ythna was sure she was going to look up and see a sarcastic leer on Jemima's sharp face, but there was none. Instead, Jemima just nodded, then walked to the window and studied the rocket they were soon going to be chained up in the belly of.

"I don't want to die in a pointless war that was lost before I was born," Ythna said.

"Really? I thought you didn't want anything, one way or the other," Jemima said, still facing the window. "Isn't that what you said? And how is this different from what would have happened to you if we had never met? You would have been sent to work for some new master, who might have worked you to death in a year or two. Or you could have been marked for Obsolescence, and died sooner. This is the same."

"It's not the same at all," Ythna said. Just when she had thought Jemima was starting to treat her like an adult.

"Isn't it?"

Ythna changed the subject. "So if everybody on board the rocket ship dies, can we use that to escape?"

"No," said Jemima. "Their deaths won't be significant. Or terribly unexpected. I can only use a single sudden death that changes lots of other people's fates."

"That's a stupid rule."

Jemima shrugged. "It's a science that won't exist for hundreds of years. Like I said: causal torsions. Think of causality as a weave that holds all of us fast, and occasionally gaps appear that you can slip through."

"So how are we going to escape before they put us on that rocket?"

"First things first." Jemima came and stood in front of Ythna, so she was silhouetted by the setting sun through the small window, and put her right hand out, palm up and at an angle. "I really do want to help. So far, all I've done is make things worse for you. If you'll let me, I'll do whatever I can. You're a smart person and you care about other people. You deserve better. And the Gaven Empire could use a million more like you."

"How does the Empire end?" Ythna said.

"It dies," Jemima said. "Everything dies eventually.

You were born in the Golden Century, which was a relatively stable era. After that, there was a twenty-year fall into decadence and social decay, followed by the Glorious Restoration, which you saw. That lasted about fifty-seven years, and was followed by the Perfect Culmination, the most exact implementation of the ideal of Dja-Thun on Earth. Which lasted about as long as you'd expect. After that, there were about a hundred and fifty years of slow decline, until the whole thing fell apart and your people begged the off-world colonists to come and save them. That's the executive summary, anyway."

"Okay," Ythna said, taking Jemima's hand in both of hers. "I want to make a difference. Give me a new identity, and put me where I can make a difference."

"Very well," Jemima said. "Done."

Jemima searched through what seemed to be a million hidden pockets sewn into the lining of her giant coat until she found a device, perhaps twice the size of your fingernail. With this gadget, she opened the lock on their cage, and then she used her tiny stun gun on the two guards in the hallway outside, who were already half asleep in any case.

"Now what?" Ythna said. "Do we wait for that

man in the helmet to arrive and murder someone else?"

"He's long gone, whoever he was," Jemima said. "But we don't need him to kill anybody. The *Dauntless* is launching tomorrow, which means I know what day this is. And someone very famous is going to die, all on his own, in the next couple days. Come on." She unlocked the front door of the holding facility with her lockpick. "We've got a lot of distance to cover. And first, we have to break out of a maximum security launch site."

Beldame Thakrra's grave wasn't nearly as fancy as the Tomb of the Unknown Emperor. They had built her a big stone sphere with a metal spike sticking through it, befitting the rank she'd attained in the moment just before she died. And there was a bust in front, with a close enough likeness of her face, except that she looked placid and sleepy, instead of keen and on the verge of asking another question. The sphere was a little taller than Ythna, and the spike soared over her head. The tomb was surrounded by other, grander memorials, as far as Ythna could see.

The sphere and the bust of Thakrra were both covered with a thick layer of grime. Nobody had visited the Beldame's tomb for decades. Maybe never. Ythna pulled a cloth out of her new, sharp-creased black uniform trousers and started to wipe the tomb so it looked fresh and clean, the way the Beldame had always kept her house. "It's good to see you again," she whispered.

Jemima came up behind Ythna while she was still wiping. "Here." She handed Ythna a stack of official-looking cards. "It's all correct. You're a Vice Officiator named Dhar. That's your name from now on. You were part of a secret mission for the Vice Emperor Htap, and everybody else who knew about that mission is dead now. Such things were common in the final days of the Perfect Culmination, sad to say. In any case, you can present these anywhere and if they need a new Vice Officiator, they'll take you on."

"Thank you," Ythna said. "But I can't go anywhere until I finish the ritual of mourning for the Beldame. I've waited much too long as it is."

"There's no rush whatsoever," Jemima said. "In fact, if I were you, I would lay low for a few more weeks before trying to travel. Oh, and if anybody asks you about the past hundred years of history, just pretend you have a head injury from that secret mission."

"What about you?" Ythna said. "Are you going to risk traveling right now?"

"Can't hang about," Jemima said. "This is the furthest forward in time I've reached in forever. And there's a death next week that I'm hopeful will send me even further ahead." She looked out at the rows of ziggurats, spheres, and statues, stretching out past the misty horizon. "I've jumped through time twenty-nine times. Twenty-nine times, and each time I find myself stuck in the Gaven Empire. There's something I'm doing wrong, and I can't figure out what it is."

"Maybe if you find that man with the helmet," Ythna said, "you can ask him."

"If I find that man again," Jemima said, "I shall have to kill him. Goodbye, Ythna. Have a great life. For me."

They embraced. Ythna watched Jemima walk away across the rows of memorials and reliquaries, the rulers and saints of the Empire resting in glory. Jemima's long black coat swished as she strode, jauntily, like someone who knew just what she was about. One arm swung back and forth, as if she had an invisible cane swatting aside the ghosts of this place. Ythna stared until all she could see was Jemima's red curls and black hat amidst the big gray shapes. Then she turned back toward the Beldame, whose stone face still looked much too complacent. Ythna wiped the bust down one more time, then sank to her knees and began the slow, mournful chant of indelible grief.

Six Months, Three Days

The man who can see the future has a date with the woman who can see many possible futures.

Judy is nervous but excited, keeps looking at things she's spotted out of the corner of her eye. She's wearing a floral Laura Ashley–style dress with an ankh necklace and her legs are rambunctious, her calves moving under the table. It's distracting because Doug knows that in two and a half weeks, those cucumber-smooth ankles will be hooked on his shoulders, and that curly reddish-brown hair will spill everywhere onto her lemon-floral pillows; this image of their future coitus has been in Doug's head for years, with varying degrees of clarity, and now it's almost here. The knowledge makes Doug almost giggle at the wrong moment, but then it hits him: she's seen this future too—or she may have, anyway.

Doug has his sandy hair cut in a neat fringe that was almost fashionable a couple years ago. You might think he cuts his own hair, but Judy knows he doesn't, because he'll tell her otherwise in a few weeks. He's much, much better looking than she thought he would be, and this comes as a huge relief. He has rude, pouty lips and an upper lip that darkens no matter how often he shaves it, with Elvis Costello glasses. And he's almost a foot taller than her, six foot four. Now that Judy's seen Doug for real, she's reimagining all the conversations they might be having in the coming weeks and months, all of the drama and all of the sweetness. The fact that Judy can be attracted to him, knowing everything that could lay ahead, consoles her tremendously.

Judy is nattering about some Chinese novelist she's been reading in translation, one of those cruel satirists from the days after the May Fourth Movement, from back when writers were so conflicted they had to rename themselves things like "Contra Diction." Doug is just staring at her, not saying anything, until it creeps her out a little.

"What?" Doug says at last, because Judy has stopped talking and they're both just staring at each other.

"You were staring at me," Judy says.

"I was . . ." Doug hesitates, then just comes out and says it. "I was savoring the moment. You know, you can know something's coming from a long way off, you know for years ahead of time the exact day and the very hour when it'll arrive. And then it arrives, and when it arrives, all you can think about is how soon it'll be gone."

"Well, I didn't know the hour and the day when you and I would meet." Judy puts a hand on his. "I saw many different hours and days. In one timeline, we would have met two years ago. In another, we'd meet a few months from now. There are plenty of timelines where we never meet at all."

Doug laughs, then waves a hand to show that he's not laughing at her, although the gesture doesn't really clarify whom or what he's actually laughing at.

Judy is drinking a cocktail called the Coalminer's Daughter, made out of ten kinds of darkness. It overwhelms her senses with sugary pungency, and leaves her lips black for a moment. Doug is drinking a wheaty pilsner from a tapered glass, in gulps. After one of them, Doug cuts to the chase. "So this is the part where I ask. I mean, I know what happens next between you and me. But here's where I ask what you think happens next."

"Well," Judy says. "There are a million tracks, you know. It's like raindrops falling into a cistern, they're separate until they hit the surface, and then they become the past: all undifferentiated. But there are an awful lot of futures where you and I date for about six months."

"Six months and three days," Doug says. "Not that I've counted or anything."

"And it ends badly."

"I break my leg."

"You break your leg ruining my bicycle. I like that bike. It's a noble five-speed in a sea of fixies."

"So you agree with me." Doug has been leaning forward, staring at Judy like a psycho again. He leans back so that the amber light spilling out of the Radish Saloon's tiny lampshades turn him the same color as his beer. "You see the same future I do." Like she's passed some kind of test.

"You didn't know what I was going to say in advance?" Judy says.

"It doesn't work like that—not for me, anyway. Remembering the future is just like remembering the past. I don't have perfect recall, I don't hang on to every detail, the transition from short-term memory to long-term memory is not always graceful."

"I guess it's like memory for me too," Judy says.

Doug feels an unfamiliar sensation, and he realizes after a while it's comfort. He's never felt this at home with another human being, especially after such a short time. Doug is accustomed to meeting people and knowing bits and pieces of their futures, from stuff he'll learn later. Or if Doug meets you and doesn't know anything about your future, that means he'll never give a crap about you, at any point down the line. This makes for awkward social interactions, either way.

They get another round of drinks. Doug gets the same beer again, Judy gets a red concoction called a Bloody Mutiny.

"So there's one thing I don't get," Doug says. "You believe you have a choice among futures—and I think you're wrong, you're seeing one true future and a bunch of false ones."

"You're probably going to spend the next six months trying to convince yourself of that," Judy says.

"So why are you dating me at all, if you get to choose? You know how it'll turn out. For that matter, why aren't you rich and famous? Why not pick a future where you win the lottery, or become a star?"

Doug works in tech support, in a poorly ventilated

subbasement of a tech company in Providence, RI, that he knows will go out of business in a couple years. He will work there until the company fails, choking on the fumes from old computers, and then be unemployed a few months.

"Well," Judy says. "It's not really that simple. I mean, the next six months, assuming I don't change my mind, they contain some of the happiest moments of my life, and I see it leading to some good things, later on. And you know, I've seen some tracks where I get rich, I become a public figure, and they never end well. I've got my eye on this one future, this one node way off in the distance, where I die aged ninety-seven, surrounded by lovers and grandchildren and cats. Whenever I have a big decision to make, I try to see the straightest path to that moment."

"So I'm a stepping stone," Doug says, not at all bitterly. He's somehow finished his second beer already, even though Judy's barely made a dent in her Bloody Mutiny.

"You're maybe going to take this journey with me for a spell," Judy says. "People aren't stones."

And then Doug has to catch the last train back to Providence, and Judy has to bike home to Somerville. Marva, her roommate, has made popcorn and hot chocolate, and wants to know the whole story.

"It was nice," Judy says. "He was a lot cuter in person than I'd remembered, which is really nice. He's tall."

"That's it?" Marva said. "Oh come on, details. You finally meet the only other freaking clairvoyant on Earth, your future boyfriend, and all you have to say is, 'He's tall.' Uh-uh. You are going to spill like a fucking oil tanker, I will ply you with hot chocolate, I may resort to Jim Beam, even."

Marva's "real" name is Martha, but she changed it years ago. She's a grad student studying eighteenth-century lit, and even Judy can't help her decide whether to finish her Ph.D. She's slightly chubby, with perfect crimson hair and clothing by Sanrio, Torrid, and Hot Topic. She is fond of calling herself "mallternative."

"I'm drunk enough already. I nearly fell off my bicycle a couple times," Judy says.

The living room is a pigsty, so they sit in Judy's room, which isn't much better. Judy hoards items she might need in one of the futures she's witnessed, and they cover every surface. There's a plastic replica of a Filipino fast food mascot, Jollibee, which she might give to this one girl Sukey in a couple of years, completing Sukey's collection and making her a friend for life—or Judy and Sukey may never meet at all. A phalanx of stuffed animals crowds Judy and Marva on the big fluffy bed. The room smells like a sachet of whoop-ass (cardamom, cinnamon, lavender) that Judy opened up earlier.

"He's a really sweet guy." Judy cannot stop talking in platitudes, which bothers her. "I mean, he's really lost, but he manages to be brave. I can't imagine what it would be like, to feel like you have no free will at all."

Marva doesn't point out the obvious thing—that Judy only sees choices for herself, not anybody else. Suppose a guy named Rocky asks Marva out on a date, and Judy sees a future in which Marva complains, afterwards, that their date was the worst evening of her life. In that case, there are two futures: One in which Judy tells Marva what she sees, and one in which she doesn't. Marva will go on the miserable date with Rocky, unless Judy tells her what she knows. (On the plus side, in fifteen months, Judy will drag Marva out to a party where she meets the love of her life. So there's that.)

"Doug's right," Marva says. "I mean, if you really have a choice about this, you shouldn't go through with it. You know it's going to be a disaster, in the end. You're the one person on Earth who can avoid the pain, and you still go sticking fingers in the socket."

"Yeah, but . . ." Judy decides this will go a lot easier if there are marshmallows in the cocoa, and runs back to the kitchen alcove. "But going out with this guy leads to good things later on. And there's a realization that I come to as a result of getting my heart broken. I come to understand something."

"And what's that?"

Judy finds the bag of marshmallows. They are stale. She decides cocoa will revitalize them and drags them back to her bedroom, along with a glass of water.

"I have no idea, honestly. That's the way with epiphanies: You can't know in advance what they'll be. Even me. I can see them coming, but I can't understand something until I understand it."

"So you're saying that the future that Doug believes is the only possible future just happens to be the best of all worlds. Is this some Leibniz shit? Does Dougie always automatically see the nicest future or something?"

"I don't think so." Judy gets gummed up by popcorn, marshmallows and sticky cocoa, and coughs her lungs out. She swigs the glass of water she brought for just this moment. "I mean—" She coughs again, and downs the rest of the water. "I mean, in Doug's version, he's only forty-three when he dies, and he's pretty broken by then. His last few years are dreadful. He tells me all about it in a few weeks."

"Wow," Marva says. "Damn. So are you going to try and save him? Is that what's going on here?"

"I honestly do not know. I'll keep you posted."

Doug, meanwhile, is sitting on his militarily neat bed, with its single hospital-cornered blanket and pillow. His apartment is almost pathologically tidy. Doug stares at his one shelf of books and his handful of carefully chosen items that play a role in his future. He chews his thumb. For the first time in years, Doug desperately wishes he had options.

He almost grabs his phone, to call Judy and tell her to get the hell away from him, because he will collapse all of her branching pathways into a dark tunnel, once and for all. But he knows he won't tell her that, and even if he did, she wouldn't listen. He doesn't love her, but he knows he will in a couple weeks, and it already hurts.

"God damnit! Fucking god fucking damn it fuck!" Doug throws his favorite porcelain bust of Wonder Woman on the floor and it shatters. Wonder Woman's head breaks into two jagged pieces, cleaving her magic tiara in half. This image, of the Amazon's raggedly bisected head, has always been in Doug's mind, whenever he's looked at the intact bust.

Doug sits a minute, dry-sobbing. Then he goes and gets his dustpan and brush.

He phones Judy a few days later. "Hey, so do you want to hang out again on Friday?"

"Sure," Judy says. "I can come down to Providence this time. Where do you want to meet up?"

"Surprise me," says Doug.

"You're a funny man."

Judy will be the second long-term relationship of Doug's life. His first was with Pamela, an artist he met in college, who made headless figurines of people who were recognizable from the neck down. (Headless Superman. Headless Captain Kirk. And yes, headless Wonder Woman, which Doug always found bitterly amusing for reasons he couldn't explain.) They were together nearly five years, and Doug never told her his secret. Which meant a lot of pretending to be surprised at stuff. Doug is used to people thinking he's kind of a weirdo.

Doug and Judy meet for dinner at one of those mom-and-pop Portuguese places in East Providence, sharing grilled squid and seared cod, with fragrant rice and a bottle of heady vinho verde. Then they walk Judy's bike back across the river towards the kinda-sorta gay bar on Wickenden Street. "The thing I like about Providence," says Doug, "is it's one of the American cities that knows its best days are behind it. So it's automatically decadent, and sort of European."

"Well," says Judy, "It's always a choice between urban decay or gentrification, right? I mean, cities aren't capable of homeostasis."

"Do you know what I'm thinking?" Doug is thinking he wants to kiss Judy. She leans up and kisses him first, on the bridge in the middle of the East Bay Bicycle Path. They stand and watch the freeway lights reflected on the water, holding hands. Everything is cold and lovely and the air smells rich.

Doug turns and looks into Judy's face, which the bridge lights have turned yellow. "I've been waiting for this moment all my life." Doug realizes he's inadvertently quoted Phil Collins. First he's mortified, then he starts laughing like a maniac. For the next half hour, Doug and Judy speak only in Phil Collins quotes.

"You can't hurry love," Judy says, which is only technically a Collins line.

Over microbrews on Wickenden, they swap origin stories, even though they already know most of it. Judy's is pretty simple: She was a little kid who overthought choices like which summer camp to go to, until she realized she could see how either decision would turn out. She still flinches when she remembers how she almost gave a valentine in third grade to Dick Petersen, who would have destroyed her. Doug's story is a lot worse: he started seeing the steps ahead, a little at a time, and then he realized his dad would die in about a year. He tried everything he could think of, for a whole year, to save his dad's life. He even buried the car keys two feet deep, on the day of his dad's accident. No fucking use.

"Turns out getting to mourn in advance doesn't make the mourning afterwards any less hard," Doug says through a beer glass snout.

"Oh man," Judy says. She knew this stuff, but hearing it is different. "I'm so sorry."

"It's okay," Doug says. "It was a long time ago."

Soon it's almost time for Judy to bike back to the train station, near that god-awful giant mall and the canal where they light the water on fire sometimes.

"I want you to try and do something for me." Judy takes Doug's hands. "Can you try to break out of the script? Not the big stuff that you think is going to happen, but just little things that you couldn't be sure about in advance if you tried. Try to surprise yourself. And maybe all those little deviations will add up to something bigger."

"I don't think it would make any difference," Doug says.

"You never know," Judy says. "There are things that I remember differently every time I think about them. Things from the past, I mean. When I was in college, I went through a phase of hating my parents, and I remembered all this stuff they did, from my childhood, as borderline abusive. And then a few years ago, I found myself recalling those same incidents again, only now they seemed totally different. Barely the same events."

"The brain is weird," Doug says.

"So you never know," Judy says. "Change the details, you may change the big picture." But she already knows nothing will come of this.

A week later, Doug and Judy lay together in her bed after having sex for the first time. It was even better than the image Doug's carried in his head since puberty. For the first time, Doug understands why people talk about sex as this transcendent thing, chains of selfhood melting away, endless abundance. They looked into each other's eyes the whole time. As for Judy, she's having that oxytocin thing she's always thought was a myth, her forehead resting on Doug's smooth chest—if she moved her head an inch she'd hear his heart beating, but she doesn't need to.

Judy gets up to pee an hour later, and when she comes back and hangs up her robe, Doug is lying there with a look of horror on his face. "What's wrong?" She doesn't want to ask, but she does anyway.

"I'm sorry." He sits up. "I'm just so happy, and . . . I can count the awesome moments in my life on a hand and a half. And I'm burning through them too fast. This is just so perfect right now. And, you know. I'm trying not to think. About."

Judy knows that if she brings up the topic they've been avoiding, they will have an unpleasant conversation. But she has to. "You have to stop this. It's obvious you can do what I do, you can see more than one branch. All you have to do is try. I know you were hurt when you were little, your dad died, and you convinced yourself that you were helpless. I'm sorry about that. But now, I feel like you're actually comfortable being trapped. You don't even try any more."

"I do." Doug is shaking. "I do try. I try every day. How dare you say I don't try."

"You don't really. I don't believe you. I'm sorry, but I don't."

"You know it's true." Doug calms down and looks Judy square in the face. Without his glasses, his eyes look as gray as the sea on a cloudy day. "The thing you told me about Marva—you always know what she's going to do. Yeah? That's how your power works. The only reason you can predict how your own choices will turn out, is because other people's actions are fixed. If you go up to some random guy on the street and slap him, you can know in advance exactly how he'll react. Right?"

"Well sure," Judy says. "I mean, that doesn't mean Marva doesn't have free will. Or this person I've hypothetically slapped." This is too weird a conversation to be having naked. She goes and puts on a Mountain Goats T-shirt and pj bottoms. "Their choices are just factored in, in advance."

"Right." Doug's point is already made, but he goes ahead and lunges for the kill. "So how do you know that I can't predict your choices, exactly the same way you can predict Marva's?"

Judy sits down on the edge of the bed. She kneads the edge of her T-shirt and doesn't look at Doug. Now she knows why Doug looked so sick when she came back from the bathroom. He saw more of this conversation than she did. "You could be right," she says after a moment. "If you're right, that makes you the one person I should never be in the same room with. I should stay the hell away from you."

"Yeah. You should," Doug says. He knows it will take forty-seven seconds before she cradles his head and kisses his forehead, and it feels like forever. He holds his breath and counts down.

A couple days later, Judy calls in sick at the arts nonprofit where she works and wanders Davis Square until she winds up in the back of the Diesel Café, in one of the plush leather booths near the pool tables. She eats one of those mint brownies that's like chocolate-covered toothpaste and drinks a lime rickey, until she feels pleasantly ill. She pulls a battered, scotch-taped world atlas out of her satchel.

She's still leafing through it a couple hours later when Marva comes and sits down opposite her.

"How did you know I was here?" Judy asks.

"Because you're utterly predictable. You said you were ditching work, and this is where you come to brood."

Judy's been single-handedly keeping the Blaze Foundation afloat for years, thanks to an uncanny knack for knowing exactly which grants to apply for and when, and what language to use on the grant proposal. She has a nearly 100 percent success rate in proposal-writing, leavened only by the fact that she occasionally applies for grants she knows she won't get. So maybe she's entitled to a sick day every now and then.

Marva sees that Judy's playing the Travel Game and joins in. She points to a spot near Madrid. "Spain," she says.

Judy's face gets all tight for a moment, like she's trying to remember where she left something. Then she smiles. "Okay, if I get on a plane to Madrid tomorrow, there are a few ways it plays out. That I can see right now. In one, I get drunk and fall off a tower and break both legs. In another, I meet this cute guy named Pedro and we have a torrid three-day affair. Then there's the one where I go to art school and study sculpture. They all end with me running out of money and coming back home."

"Malawi," Marva says. Judy thinks for a moment, then remembers what happens if she goes to Malawi tomorrow.

"This isn't as much fun as usual," Marva says after they've gone to Vancouver and Paris and Sao Paolo. "Your heart isn't in it."

"It's not," Judy says. "I just can't see a happy future where I don't date Doug. I mean, I like Doug, I may even be in love with him already, but . . . we're going to break each other's hearts, and more than that: We're maybe going to break each other's *spirits*.

There's got to be a detour, a way to avoid this, but I just can't see it right now."

Marva dumps a glass of water on Judy's head.

"Wha? You— Wha?" She splutters like a cartoon duck.

"Didn't see that coming, did you?"

"No, but that doesn't mean . . . I mean, I'm not freaking omniscient, I sometimes miss bits and pieces, you know that."

"I am going to give you the Samuel Johnson/ Bishop Berkeley lecture, for like the tenth time," Marva says. "Because sometimes, a girl just needs a little Johnson."

Bishop George Berkeley, of course, was the "if a tree falls in the forest and nobody hears it, does it make a sound" guy, who argued that objects only exist in our perceptions. One day, Boswell asked Samuel Johnson what he thought of Berkeley's idea. According to Boswell, Johnson's response to this was to kick a big rock "with mighty force," saying, "I refute it thus."

"The point," says Marva, "is that nobody can see everything. Not you, not Doug, not Bishop Berkeley. Stuff exists that your senses can't perceive and your mind can't comprehend. Even if you do have an extra sense the rest of us don't have. Okay? So don't get all doom and gloom on me. Just remember:

Would Samuel Johnson have let himself feel trapped in a dead-end relationship?"

"Well, considering he apparently dated a guy named Boswell who went around writing down everything he said . . . I really don't know." Judy runs to the bathroom to put her head under the hot-air dryer.

The next few weeks, Judy and Doug hang out at least every other day and grow accustomed to kissing and holding hands all the time, trading novelty for the delight of positive reinforcement. They're at the point where their cardiovascular systems crank into top gear if one of them sees someone on the street who even looks, for a second, like the other. Doug notices little things about Judy that catch him off guard, like the way she rolls her eyes slightly before she's about to say something solemn. Judy realizes that Doug's joking on some level, most of the time, even when he seems tragic. Maybe especially then.

They fly a big dragon kite on Cambridge Common, with a crimson tail. They go to the Isabella Stewart Gardner, and sip tea in the courtyard. Once or twice, Doug is about to turn left, but Judy stops him, because something way cooler will happen if they go right instead. They discuss which kind of skylight Batman prefers to burst through when he breaks into criminals' lairs, and whether Batman ever uses the chimney like Santa Claus. They break down the taxonomy of novels where Emily Dickinson solves murder mysteries.

Marva gets used to eating Doug's spicy omelettes, which automatically make him Judy's best-ever boyfriend in Marva's book. Marva walks out of her bedroom in the mornings to see Doug wearing the bathrobe Judy got for him, flipping a perfect yellow slug over and over, and she's like, What *are* you? To Marva, the main advantage of making an omelette is that when it falls apart halfway through, you can always claim you planned to make a scramble all along.

Judy and Doug enjoy a couple months of relative bliss, based on not ever discussing the future. In the back of her mind, Judy never stops looking for the break point, the moment where a timeline splits off from the one Doug believes in. It could be just a split second.

They reach their three-month anniversary, roughly the midpoint of their relationship. To celebrate, they take a weekend trip to New York together, and they wander down Broadway and all around the Village and Soho. Doug is all excited, showing off for once—he points out the fancy restaurant where the President will be assassinated in 2027, and the courthouse where Lady Gaga gets arrested for civil disobedience right after she wins the Nobel Peace Prize. Judy has to keep shushing him. Then she gives in, and the two of them loudly debate whether the election of 2024 will be rigged, not caring if people stare.

Once they've broken the taboo on talking about the future in general, Doug suddenly feels free to talk about their future, specifically. They're having a romantic dinner at one of those restaurant/bars, with high-end American food and weird pseudo-Soviet iconography everywhere. Doug is on his second beer when he says, "So, I guess in a couple of weeks, you and I have that ginormous fight about whether I should meet your parents. And about a week after that, I manage to offend Marva. Honestly, without meaning to. But then again, in a month and a half's time, we have that really nice day together on the boat."

"Please don't," Judy says, but she already knows it's too late to stop it.

"And then after that, there's the Conversation. I am not looking forward to the Conversation."

"We both know about this stuff," Judy says. "It'll

happen if and when it happens, why worry about it until then?"

"Sorry, it's just part of how I deal with things. It helps me to brace myself."

Judy barely eats her entrée. Doug keeps oversharing about their next few months, like a floodgate has broken. Some of it's stuff Judy either didn't remember, or has blotted out of her mind because it's so dismal. She can tell Doug's been obsessing about every moment of the coming drama, visualizing every incident until it snaps into perfect focus.

By the time Judy gets up and walks away from the table, she sees it all just as clearly as he does. She can't even imagine any future other than the one he's described. Doug's won.

Judy roams Bleecker and St. Mark's Place, until she claims a small victory: She realizes that if she goes into this one little subterranean bar, she'll run into a cute guy she hasn't seen since high school, and they'll have a conversation in which he confesses that he always had a crush on her back then. Because Doug's not there, he's not able to tell her whether she goes into that bar or not. She does, and she's late getting back to their hotel, even though she and cute high-school guy don't do anything but talk.

Doug makes an effort to be nice the rest of the

weekend, even though he knows it won't do him any good, except that Judy holds hands with him on the train back to Providence and Boston.

And then Doug mentions, in passing, that he'll see Judy around, after they break up—including two meetings a decade from now, and one time a full fifteen years hence, and he knows some stuff. He starts to say more, but Judy runs to the dining car, covering her ears.

When the train reaches Doug's stop and he's gathering up his stuff, Judy touches his shoulder. "Listen, I don't know if you and I actually do meet up in a decade, it's a blur to me right now. But I don't want to hear whatever you think you know. Okay?" Doug nods.

When the fight over whether Doug should meet Judy's parents arrives, it's sort of a meta-fight. Judy doesn't see why Doug should do the big parental visit, since Judy and Doug are scheduled to break up in ten weeks. Doug just wants to meet them because he wants to meet them—maybe because his own parents are dead. And he's curious about these people who are aware that their daughter can see the future(s). They compromise, as expected: Doug meets Judy's parents over lunch when they visit, and he's on his best behavior.

They take a ferry out to sea, toward Block Island. The air is too cold and they feel seasick and the sun blinds them, and it's one of the greatest days of their lives. They huddle together on deck and when they can see past the glare and the sea spray and they're not almost hurling, they see the glimmer of the ocean, streaks of white and blue and yellow in different places, as the light and wind affect it. The ocean feels utterly forgiving, like you can dump almost anything into the ocean's body and it will still love us, and Judy and Doug cling to each other like children in a storm cellar and watch the waves. Then they go to Newport and eat amazing lobster. For a few days before and a few days after this trip, they are all aglow and neither of them can do any wrong.

A week or so after the boat thing, they hold hands in bed, nestling like they could almost start having sex at any moment. Judy looks in Doug's naked eyes (his glasses are on the nightstand) and says, "Let's just jump off the train now, okay? Let's not do any of the rest of it, let's just be good to each other forever. Why not? We could."

"Why would you want that?" Doug drawls like he's half asleep. "You're the one who's going to get the life she wants. I'm the one who'll be left like wreckage." Judy rolls over and pretends to sleep.

The Conversation achieves mythical status long before it arrives. Certain aspects of The Conversation are hazy in advance, for both Doug and Judy, because of that thing where you can't understand something until you understand it.

The day of the Conversation, Judy wakes from a nightmare, shivering with the covers cast aside, and Doug's already out of bed. "It's today," he says, and then he leaves without saying anything else to Judy, or anything at all to Marva, who's still pissed at him. Judy keeps almost going back to bed, but somehow she winds up dressed, with a toaster pop in her hand, marching towards the door. Marva starts to say something, then shrugs.

Doug and Judy meet up for dinner at Punjabi Dhaba in Inman Square, scooping red-hot eggplant and bright chutney off of metal prison trays while Bollywood movies blare overhead and just outside of their line of vision.

The Conversation starts with them talking past each other. Judy says, "Lately I can't remember anything past the next month." Doug says, "I keep trying to see what happens after I die." Judy says, "Normally I can remember years in advance, even decades. But I'm blocked." She shudders. Doug says, "If I could just have an impression, an afterimage, of what happens when I'm gone. It would help a lot."

Judy finally hears what Doug's been saying. "Oh Jesus, not this. Nobody can see past death. It's impossible."

"So's seeing the future." Doug cracks his somosa in half with a fork, and offers the chunky side to Judy.

"You can't remember anything past when your brain ceases to exist. Because there are no physical memories to access. Your brain is a storage medium."

"But who knows what we're accessing? It could be something outside our own brains."

Judy tries to clear her head and think of something nice twenty years from now, but she can't. She looks at Doug's chunky sideburns, which he didn't have when they'd started dating. Whenever she's imagined those sideburns, she always associated them with the horror of these days. It's sweltering inside the restaurant. "Why are you scared of me?" she says.

"I'm not," Doug says. "I only want you to be happy. When I see you ten years from now, I—"

Judy covers her ears and jumps out of her seat, to turn the Bollywood music all the way up. Standing, she can see the screen, where a triangle of dancing women shake their fingers in unison at an unshaven man. The man smiles.

Eventually, someone comes and turns the music back down. "I think part of you is scared that I really am more powerful than you are," Judy says. "And you've done everything you can to take away my power."

"I don't think you're any more or less powerful than me. Our powers are just different," Doug says. "But I think you're a selfish person. I think you're used to the idea that you can cheat on everything, and it's made your soul a little bit rotten. I think you're going to hate me for the next few weeks until you figure out how to cast me out. I think I love you more than my own arms and legs and I would shorten my already short life by a decade to have you stick around one more year. I think you're brave as hell for keeping your head up on our journey together into the mouth of hell. I think you're the most beautiful human being I've ever met, and you have a good heart despite how much you're going to tear me to shreds."

"I don't want to see you any more," Judy says. Her hair is all in her face, wet and ragged from the restaurant's blast-furnace heat.

A few days later, Judy and Doug are playing foozball at a swanky bar in what used to be the Combat Zone. Judy makes a mean remark about something sexually humiliating that will happen to Doug five years from now, which he told her about in a moment of weakness. A couple days later, she needles him about an incident at work that almost got him fired a while back. She's never been a sadist before now—although it's also masochism, because when she torments him, she already knows how terrible she'll feel in a few minutes.

Another time, Doug and Judy are drunk on the second floor of a Thayer Street frat bar, and Doug keeps getting Judy one more weird cocktail, even though she's had more than enough. The retro pinball machine gossips at them. Judy staggers to the bathroom, leaving her purse with Doug—and when she gets back, the purse is gone. They both knew Doug was going to lose Judy's purse, which only makes her madder. She bitches him out in front of a table of beer-pong champions. And then it's too late to get back to Judy's place, so they have to share Doug's cramped, sagging hospital cot. Judy throws up on Doug's favorite outfit: anise and stomach acid, it'll never come out.

Judy loses track of which unbearable things have already happened, and which lay ahead. Has Doug insulted her parents yet, on their second meeting? Yes, that was yesterday. Has he made Marva cry? No, that's tomorrow. Has she screamed at him that he's a weak mean bastard yet? It's all one moment to her. Judy has finally achieved timelessness.

Doug has already arranged—a year ago—to take two weeks off work, because he knows he won't be able to answer people's dumb tech problems and lose a piece of himself at the same time. He could do his job in his sleep, even if he didn't know what all the callers were going to say before they said it, but his ability to sleepwalk through unpleasantness will shortly be maxed out. He tells his coworker Geoffrey, the closest he has to a friend, that he'll be doing some Spring cleaning, even though it's October.

A few days before the breakup, Judy stands in the middle of Central Square, and a homeless guy comes up to her and asks for money. She stares at his face, which is unevenly sunburned in the shape of a wheel. She concentrates on this man, who stands there, his hand out. For a moment, she just forgets to worry about Doug for once—and just like that, she's seeing futures again.

The threads are there: if she buys this homeless man some scones from 1369, they'll talk, and become friends, and maybe she'll run into him once every few weeks and buy him dinner, for the next several years. And in five years, she'll help the man, Franklin, find a place to live, and she'll chip in for the deposit. But a couple years later, it'll all have fallen apart, and he'll be back here. And she flashes on something Franklin tells her eight years from now, if this whole chain of events comes to pass, about a lost opportunity. And then she knows what to do.

"Franklin," she says to wheel-faced guy, who blinks at the sound of his name. "Listen. Angie's pregnant, with your kid. She's at the yellow house with the broken wheelbarrow, in Sturbridge. If you go to her right now, I think she'll take you back. Here's a hundred bucks." She reaches in her new purse, for the entire wad of cash she took out of the bank to hold her until she gets her new ATM card. "Go find Angie." Franklin just looks at her, takes the cash, and disappears.

Judy never knows if Franklin took her advice. But she does know for sure she'll never see him again.

And then she wanders into the bakery where she would have bought Franklin scones, and she sees this guy working there. And she concentrates on him, too, even though it gives her a headache, and she "remembers" a future in which they become friendly and he tells her about the time he wrecked his best friend's car, which hasn't happened yet. She buys a scone and tells the guy, Scott, that he shouldn't borrow Reggie's T-Bird for that regatta thing, or he'll regret it forever. She doesn't even care that Scott is staring as she walks out.

"I'm going to be a vigilante soothsayer," she tells Marva. She's never used her power so recklessly before, but the more she does it, the easier it gets. She goes ahead and mails that Jollibee statue to Sukey.

The day of the big breakup, Marva's like, "Why can't you just dump him via text message? That's what all the kids are doing, it's the new sexting." Judy's best answer is, "Because then my bike would still be in one piece." Which isn't a very good argument. Judy dresses warm, because she knows she'll be frozen later.

Doug takes deep breaths, tries to feel acceptance, but he's all wrung out inside. He wants this to be over, but he dreads it being over. If there was any other way . . . Doug takes the train from Providence a couple hours early, so he can get lost for a while. But he doesn't get lost enough, and he's still early for their meeting. They're supposed to get dinner at the fancy place, but Doug forgot to make the reservation, so they wind up at John Harvard's Brew Pub, in the mall, and they each put away three pints of the microbrews that made John Harvard famous. They make small talk.

Afterwards, they're wandering aimlessly, towards Mass Ave., and getting closer to the place where it happens. Judy blurts out, "It didn't have to be this way. None of it. You made everything fall into place, but it didn't have to."

"I know you don't believe that any more," Doug says. "There's a lot of stuff you have the right to blame me for, but you can't believe I chose any of this. We're both cursed to see stuff that nobody should be allowed to see, but we're still responsible for our own mistakes. I still don't regret anything. Even if I didn't know today was the last day for you and me, I would want it to be."

They are both going to say some vicious things to each other in the next hour or so. They've already heard it all, in their heads.

On Mass Ave., Judy sees the ice cream place opposite the locked side gates of Harvard, and she stops her bike. During their final blow-out fight, she's not eating ice cream, any of the hundred times she's seen it. "Watch my bike," she tells Doug. She goes in and gets a triple scoop for herself and one for Doug, random flavors—Cambridge is one of the few places you can ask for random flavors and people will just nod—and then she and Doug resume their exit interview.

"It's that you have this myth that you're totally innocent and harmless, even though you also believe you control everything in the universe," Doug is saying.

Judy doesn't taste her ice cream, but she is aware of its texture, the voluptuousness of it, and the way it chills the roof of her mouth. There are lumps of something chewy in one of her random flavors. Her cone smells like candy, with a hint of wet dog.

They wind up down by the banks of the river, near the bridge surrounded by a million geese and their innumerable droppings, and Judy is crying and shouting that Doug is a passive-aggressive asshole.

Doug's weeping into the remains of his cone, and then he goes nuclear. He starts babbling about when he sees Judy ten years hence, and the future he describes is one of the ones that Judy's always considered somewhat unlikely.

Judy tries to flee, but Doug has her wrist and he's babbling at her, describing a scene where a broken-down Doug meets Judy with her two kids—Raina and Jeremy, one of dozens of combinations of kids Judy might have—and Raina, the toddler, has a black eye and a giant stuffed tiger. The future Judy looks tired, makes an effort to be nice to the future Doug, who's a wreck, gripping her cashmere lapel.

Both the future Judy and the present Judy are trying to get away from Doug as fast as possible. Neither Doug will let go.

"And then fifteen years from now, you only have one child," Doug says.

"Let me go!" Judy screams.

But when Judy finally breaks free of Doug's hand, and turns to flee, she's hit with a blinding headrush, like a one-minute migraine. Three scoops of ice cream on top of three beers, or maybe just stress, but it paralyzes her, even as she's trying to run. Doug tries to throw himself in her path, but he overbalances and falls down the riverbank, landing almost in the water.

"Gah!" Doug wails. "Help me up. I'm hurt." He lifts one arm, and Judy puts down her bike, helps him climb back up. Doug's a mess, covered with mud, and he's clutching one arm, heaving with pain.

"Are you okay?" Judy can't help asking.

"Breaking my arm hurt a lot more . . ." Doug winces. ". . . than I thought it would."

"Your arm." Judy can't believe what she's seeing. "You broke . . . your arm."

"You can see for yourself. At least this means it's over."

"But you were supposed to break your leg."

Doug almost tosses both hands in the air, until he remembers he can't. "This is exactly why I can't deal with you any more. We both agreed, on our very first date, I break my arm. You're just remembering it wrong, or being difficult on purpose."

Doug wants to go to the hospital by himself, but Judy insists on going with. He curses at the pain, stumbling over every knot and root.

"You broke your arm." Judy's half-sobbing, half-laughing, it's almost too much to take in. "You broke your arm, and maybe that means that all of this . . . that maybe we could try again. Not right away, I'm feeling pretty raw right now, but in a while. I'd be willing to try."

But she already knows what Doug's going to say: "You don't get to hurt me any more."

She doesn't leave Doug until he's safely staring at the hospital linoleum, waiting to go into X-ray. Then she pedals home, feeling the cold air smash into her face. She's forgotten her helmet, but it'll be okay. When she gets home, she's going to grab Marva and they're going straight to Logan, where a bored check-in counter person will give them dirt-cheap tickets on the last flight to Miami. They'll have the wildest three days of their lives, with no lasting ill effects. It'll be epic, she's already living every instant of it in her head. She's crying buckets but it's okay, her bike's headwind wipes the slate clean.

Clover

The day after Anwar and Joe got married, a man showed up on their doorstep with a cat hunched in the cradle of his arms. The man was short and thin, almost child-size, with a pale, weathered face. The cat was black, with a white streak on his stomach and a white slash on his face. The man congratulated them on their nuptials, and held out the squirming cat. "This is Berkley," he said. "If you take him into your home, you'll have nine years of good luck."

Before Anwar and Joe had a chance to debate the matter of adoption, Berkley was already hiding in their apartment somewhere. They found themselves Googling the closest place to get a cat bed, a litter box, and some grain-free, low-fat organic food for an indoor cat. It was a chilly day, with scattered clouds that turned the sunset into a broken yolk.

Berkley didn't come out of hiding for a month. Food disappeared from his bowl, and his litter box filled up, when nobody was looking. But the cat himself was a no-show. Until one night, when Anwar had a nightmare that the tanks cracked and his precious, life-giving beer sprayed everywhere. He woke to find the cat perched on the side of the bed, eyes lit up, one leg outstretched. Anwar froze for a moment, then tentatively reached out an arm and touched the cat's back so lightly the fur lifted. Then Berkley scooted in next to Anwar and fell asleep, thrumming slightly. From then on, Berkley slept on their bed at night.

Their luck didn't become miraculous or anything, but things did go well for them. Anwar's microbrews grew popular, especially Nubian Nut and Butch Goddess, and he even managed to open a small brewpub, an "airy cavern" in the trendy warehouse district between NC State and downtown, not far from where there used to be that leather bar. Joe documented a couple of major atrocities without becoming a statistic himself, and wrote a white paper about genocide that he really felt might could make genocides a bit less likely. Anwar and Joe stayed together, and Joe's hand along Anwar's lower ribs always made him feel safe and amazed. Everyone they knew was suffering—like Marie, whose restaurant went under because she couldn't get half the ingredients she needed due to the drought, and then she went back to Ohio to care for an uncle who'd gotten the antibiotic-resistant meningitis, and wound up getting sick herself. But Anwar and Joe kept being good to each other, and when problems came, they muddled through.

They almost didn't notice the upcoming ninth anniversary of Berkley's arrival. By now, the cat was the defining feature of their home, the lodestone. Berkley's moods were their household's moods: his pleasure, their pleasure. They went across town to get him the exact food he wanted, and kept him well supplied with toys and cat grass, not to mention an enormous climbing tree. Anwar's most popular stout was the Black Cat's Tail.

Nine years after Berkley's arrival, to the day, another man showed up at their door, with another cat. A female this time, a fluffy calico with an intense glare in her wide yellow eyes. This cat did not squirm or fidget, but instead had a wary stillness.

"This is Patricia," the big bearded lumbersexual white dude said without introducing himself. "You won't have any extra luck if you take her in, but she'll be a good companion for Berkley." He deposited her on their doorstep and skipped away before Anwar or Joe had a chance to ask any questions.

They decided "Patricia" was an odd name for a cat, and named her "Clover" instead, because of the pattern of the spots on her back.

Berkley had worked for years to get Anwar and Joe's apartment under control, and this represented both a creative enterprise and a labor of love. He had carved out cozy beds atop the laundry hamper, inside the old wicker basket that contained extra brewing supplies, and in the hutch where Joe kept his beloved death-metal concert shirts. Berkley knew exactly where the sunbeam came through the slanty front windows in the mornings, and the best hiding places for when Anwar brought out the terrifying vacuum-cleaner monster versus when Anwar and Joe started shouting after Joe came home from one of his trips. Berkley had trained both men to sleep in exactly the right positions for him to curl up between their legs.

And now this new cat, this jag-faced maniac, sprinted around the front room, the bedroom, the kitchenette, the bathrooms—even the laundry nook! She trampled everything with her wild feet. She put her scent everywhere. She slept on the sofa, where Joe sat and stroked her shiny fur with both hands. She was just all over everything.

Berkley made no secret of his feelings on the subject of this invasion. His oratorio spanned two octaves and had an infinite number of movements. But his pleas and remonstrations went unheeded, as if his companionship were a faded, shredded old toy that had lost all its scent. Berkley should have known. This was the way of things: You get a sweet deal for a while, but just when you get comfortable, someone always comes and rips it away.

This lesson, Berkley had learned as a kitten. His first proper human had been a young girl who had sworn to protect him, and Berkley had promised to watch over her in turn. Somehow, they had struck this deal in the language of cats, which made it much larger than the usual declarations that cats and people always make to each other. And then, she had disappeared.

Berkley never knew what had happened, only that he'd had a friend, and then she was gone. He was left alone in this giant wooden house, where every smell was a doorway. He'd searched for her over and over, his tail down and his head upcast. He had cried much too loud for his own good. There were still people in that house, but they didn't love Berkley, or even wish him well. Their angry shouts and stomping boots echoed off the ancient walls, ever since Berkley's friend disappeared. Every time he emerged from hiding to call out to his lost friend, he risked getting plucked off his feet by grabby hands.

He kept thinking he heard her or smelled her, but no. This always set off the wailing again.

Quick quick quick sleep.

Quick quick quick sleep.

Sometimes the grabby hands caught him, and then his hard-gotten dignity was all undone. His body bent into shapes where it didn't want to go.

They heard Berkley cry, the angry people, and they shouted, they pounded the walls. He didn't have a way to stop crying.

Friend didn't mean to Berkley the same thing it would to a dog, or a human. But this girl had been the shoulder he slept on, the hand that scritched his ear, the voice that sang to him. Even the cozy old attic felt colder and darker, and the wooden house smelled like nothing but mildew.

Berkley was just letting go of the last of his kittenhood when another pair of hands had lifted him, gently, and brought him to this new house, where the scents were different (yeast, flowers, nuts) but the people were kind. Berkley forgot almost everything in life, but he never entirely forgot the girl, his original disappointment.

And just like the girl had been taken away from Berkley with zero warning or goodbye, now this new cat was going to steal all his comfort from him. Clover tried to talk to him a few times, but he was having exactly none of that. Berkley hissed at her like she was made of poison.

The thing was, Anwar really believed, deep down, in the "nine years of good luck." He always referred to Berkley as their *maneki neko*, like one of those Japanese cat statues that waves a paw in the window and brings in good fortune. When the second guy showed up exactly nine years later, with another cat, and he knew so much, that clinched it.

Anwar had a sick feeling: *Our luck just ran out.*

Raleigh was an okay friendly city, mostly, but lately when he found himself downtown at night, he felt like he was going to get jumped any minute. Big scary dudes had followed him out to his truck from the bar once or twice, but Anwar had always gotten away. The mosque in Durham had gotten graffitied, and the gay bar off I-40, bricked. Inside his own bar, Anwar was getting more ignorant tipsy people up in his face, asking why he was brewing alcoholic drinks anyway—when, hello, the Egyptians *invented* beer, thank you very much. The barback, a large Hungarian named Vinnie, had needed to eject more and more abusive drunks recently. Anwar didn't want to live in fear, so instead, he lived in the sweet spot between paranoia and rage.

The one-bedroom apartment, with its scuffed hardwood floors, crimson drapes, and shelves sagging with ancient books, seemed like a refuge. Locking the door from the inside, Anwar always took a deep breath, like his lungs were expanding to the size of the stucco walls. He felt ten years older outdoors than indoors.

But lately, Joe woke up angry, because funding cuts, and he was constantly having to haul ass up to D.C. for crisis strategy meetings. When Joe was home, and not crashing at Roddy's place near Adams Morgan, he was a piece of driftwood in the bed, rigid and spiky. Joe talked to a point somewhere to the left of Anwar, instead of looking straight at him. The cats had gone to ground, as if sensing a high-pressure front: Berkley in one of his thousand hiding places, Clover under the sofa. Anwar screwed up his hamstring and limped around the apartment, and when he ventured outside it was with a *what now* feeling—maybe this time his truck wouldn't start, or the neighbors would have a campaign sign for that guy who insisted North Carolina would never accept refugees from any of the places where Joe kept track of atrocities.

"You got the right idea, staying home all the time," Anwar told Berkley, who grudgingly offered his white tummy.

So one day, Anwar got done showering, and all the real towels were dirty. So he dried off using a hand towel. He emerged from the bathroom, cupping himself in that small woolen square, and saw Joe staring at him, gray eyes wide and unwavering. Anwar felt himself blush, was about to say something flirtatious to his husband, but Joe was turning to close the half-open front curtain, where anybody could see in from the front stoop.

"You might want to do a *lot* more crunches before you pose in front of an open window like that."

Anwar bit his own tongue so hard his mouth filled up with blood. He just backed away—first into the bathroom, but there was nothing to cover him there, so he took a hard left into the bedroom. Still limping, he nearly stepped on Clover, who ran to get out of his way. Joe might as well have broken that window instead of covering it.

"Hey, I didn't mean . . ." Joe came in just as Anwar

was pulling on his baggiest pants. "You know I think you're beautiful. I just meant, the neighbors. I was just teasing. That came out all wrong. I didn't mean it like that."

"Don't you have a meeting in D.C. to get to?"

Once Joe was gone, Anwar fell onto the sofa, wearing just his big sweatpants. He felt gross. All of Joe's previous relationships had ended with some combination of sarcasm and distraction, but Anwar always thought he'd be different. Anwar looked at his forearms, which at least were buff, thanks to pouring so much beer. He had to be there in a few hours, unless he called in sick.

Clover had jumped on the sofa when Anwar wasn't looking, and had scrunched next to him with her head resting on his thigh. He scritched her head with one hand and she purred, while Berkley glared from the opposite end of the room. "Hey, it's not your fault our luck went south when you showed up," he told her. "I'm sorry you had to see us like this. We were a lot cooler when everything was going our way."

The cat looked up at him with her eyes perfect yellow spheres, except for tiny black slits, and said, "Oh, shit."

Then she sprang upright. "Shit! I'm a cat. WTF.

I didn't mean for this to . . . how long have I been a cat? This is really bad. You have to help me, or I'm going to get stuck like this. Listen, do you have a phone? I need you to dial for me, because I have no freaking opposable digits. Listen, it's—"

Then Clover stopped talking, abruptly. She sat down, looked up at him, and let out a long, high chirp, like the sound a cat makes when it's sitting at an open window and trying to communicate with passing birds.

Berkley's life was ruined, and it felt worse than the first time. He was a lot older this time, and, too, he couldn't run and hide from this.

Joe was gone. As in, just not at home anymore—he had been around less and less, lately, but now days had passed without his scent or his voice. Anwar was still there, but he wasn't acting like Anwar. No gentle pats, no tug-of-war with the catnip banana. No silly noises. The only cat that Anwar paid attention to was Clover, and he acted as if Clover had quit in the middle of playing a game that Anwar really wanted to continue.

It was way past time someone sent Clover to The Vet.

Berkley was a fierce, crafty hunter. He found the

perfect bookshelf from which to watch for Clover emerging from under the sofa. She usually came out when the mail rained down from the slot in the front door, because that was like a daily miracle: paper from the skies! Berkley had a claw, ready to swipe.

He almost got her. She ducked out of the way, just as the claw came down, and he caught some dust mites instead. She ran, back toward the sofa, and he followed.

"New cat!" he hissed at her. "You ruined it all!"

"I didn't mean to!"

As Berkley stalked her, he found himself telling her the story of his original disappointment: how he'd lived in an old wooden house with a cruel girl and a strange girl. And Berkley had made the strange girl his own, until she was taken away, and he was left worse than before. That "worse than before" was where Berkley was, now, and he had nothing left but to share that feeling with Clover.

"But," Clover said from under the sofa, "that was me. *I* was the weird girl. I remember now. I promised to protect you. I kept my promise! That's how you got here. I kept my promise. And now I need you to help me in return."

And just like that, Clover lost her fear of Berkley.

She talked her wild talk at him, out in the open, and no amount of claw-swipes could scare her off. As mad as she was acting, it was almost like she *wanted* to go to The Vet.

"I was a person. I lived with you," Clover kept saying. "I went away to learn more tricks. I could speak cat, sometimes, but I wanted to do more. But when I left, I thought about you all the time. I had bad dreams about you. Scary dreams. I imagined you all alone in that old house, with my family, and I had to save you. But my teachers wouldn't let me leave the school. So I asked them to save you."

Berkley growled. "So then you just told a man to come and take me away? That was all you did?"

"They said they found you the perfect home, the best family for you. They said I could repay them later. I didn't understand what they meant. But now! I have to turn back into a person soon, or I will just lose myself. I don't know how. I think this is a test, and I'm failing it. You have to help me. Please!"

Berkley considered this for a moment. "So. You say you are the girl who abandoned me as a kitten, and spoiled my good thing. And now you've come back as a cat, to spoil my good thing a second time. And you want *me* to help *you*?" Berkley let out the most disdainful, vengeful hiss that he possibly could, then turned and walked away without looking back.

Anwar had met Joe at this death-metal concert that his friends had dragged him to, in a beer-slick dark club that resembled the inside of a giant van. When he saw Joe in his torn denim and tank top waiting at the bar, his heart had just flipped, and he'd stood next to Joe for ten minutes before he got up the nerve to say hi. Their first three dates, Anwar lied his ass off and pretended to be a death-metal fan, to the point where he had to keep sneaking away to text his friends with questions about Finnish musicians. Joe had this mane of red hair and permanent five-o'clock shadow flecked with white, and a way of talking about guitar solos that was way better than listening to music.

When Joe had found out that Anwar actually loathed metal, he'd nearly wept. "Nobody's ever done anything like that for me. That is so . . . beautiful." He kissed Anwar so hard, Anwar tasted whiskey and felt Joe's stubble on the corners of his mouth. That's when Anwar knew this was the man he wanted to marry.

Joe was Anwar's first real, proper love. But Joe was more than a decade older, and had already lived through a string of two-year and three-year relationships. Joe had experienced enough relationship failure to be inured. When they'd first hooked up, Joe had prized Anwar's twenty-something body, his lean golden frame, and seeing that covetous look in the eyes of this slightly grizzled rocker dude had punched a button Anwar didn't even know he had.

Anwar prized Joe's independence, the way he always said, *Live like the fuckers don't own you,* even after they went all domestic together. His gentleness, even when he was pissed off, and the warm sound of his voice when he checked in. Joe had not checked in in ages—they had barely even talked on the phone—because the emergency in D.C. had given birth to other emergencies, and now there was a whole emergency extended family.

Meanwhile, Anwar's truck kept not starting, there was a weird stain on the bathroom wall, and, well, Anwar was losing his mind and imagining that his cat had talked to him. Clover hadn't spoken since that one time, but she'd been on a tear: chasing Berkley around, making weird noises, knocking things over. Both cats were upset, since Joe was gone and Anwar wasn't himself. Anwar kept trying to pull himself together and at least be there for these two furballs, but he only stayed together for a minute or two at a time, no matter how hard he tried.

Then another one of those men showed up at his door: this one pale and thin, with elaborate tattoos on his hands, and a dark suit with a thin tie. "Don't mind me," the man said. "I just want to talk to your cat." Anwar stepped aside and let the man come in.

"How was the good luck, by the way?" The man peered under various pieces of furniture, looking for Clover. "Were you happy with how it turned out?"

"Um, it was okay, I guess," Anwar said. "I'm still trying to decide, to be honest." He wanted to say more—like maybe he and Joe had never been tested, as a couple, because everything had gone so smoothly for them until now. Maybe they'd have been stronger if they hadn't had training wheels. Maybe they were just fair-weather lovers.

"Okeydoke," the man said. "I could get you another dose of luck, but it would cost a lot more this time." He squatted in front of the sofa, where Clover eyed him. "Has she talked to you?"

"Um," Anwar said. "I guess so. Yes."

"Don't believe anything she says." The man reached out a hand gently, and Clover let him pet her, fingers under the chin. "She's the worst combination of congenital liar and delusional. Even she doesn't always know if she's telling the truth."

"So she was lying when she told me that she used to be a person?"

"No, that was true. She wanted me to do her a favor, and this was the result." The man snapped his fingers in front of Clover's face. "Come on, then. What do you have to say for yourself?" *Snap, snap.* "How's the food?" *Snap.* "Are you enjoying your accommodations?"

Clover just stared at him and grumbled a little. She twitched whenever he snapped his fingers, but she didn't try to run away.

"Either she's unable to speak, because she just hasn't gotten it under control, or she's just being pissy. Either way, disappointing." The man stood up. "Please let me know if she speaks to you again." He handed Anwar a business card that just had a Meeyu handle. "And if you decide you need another lucky break, just @ me."

"What exactly would I have to do to get more good luck?"

"It really depends. Some of it might be stuff where you wouldn't really be you by the end of it. But I tell you what, if you can get that cat speaking English again, that would go a long way."

The man spun on one heel, almost like one of Joe's old dance moves, and walked out the door without saying goodbye or closing the door behind him. Anwar hated when anyone left the door open, even for a second, because he never wanted the cats to get any ideas.

Joe called when Anwar was in the middle of trying to coax words out of Clover with cat treats and recitations of Sufi poetry. (No dice.) "Things are beyond crazy, you have no idea. I'm trying to come back to you but every time I think I'm going to get out of here, there's another fucking drama eruption. The auditors are maniacs." In the background, Anwar could hear guitar heroics and laughing voices. "I am going to make it up to you, I swear. I still have to apologize properly for being such an ass before. I gotta go." Joe hung up before Anwar could even say anything.

Anwar had sort of wanted to ask Joe if he felt like they'd been lucky, these past nine years, and whether the luck would be worth going to extremes to get back. But he couldn't think of a way to ask such a thing.

Berkley took a wild skittering run from one end of the apartment to the other, and just as he hit peak speed, he reached the front door, where Clover was sitting waiting for the mail to rain down. He vaulted over her, paws passing almost within shredding distance, and landed at the front door, so hard the mail slot rattled.

Clover just looked at him, eyes partway hooded.

Berkley pulled into a crouch, ready to spring, claws out, ready to tear the new cat apart. But that bored look in her eyes made him stop before he jumped. He was a cunning hunter. He could wait for his moment. She hadn't talked any more nonsense to Berkley since that one time, but she still didn't seem scared of him. He didn't know what he was dealing with.

"New cat," Berkley said in a low voice. "I'm going to send you to The Vet."

Clover didn't reply. The mail fell, but it was just a single envelope with red shapes on it.

Some time later, Anwar cried into his knees on the couch. He smelled wrong—pungent and kind of rotten, instead of like nice soap and hops. He was all shrunk inward, in the opposite of the ready-to-pounce stance that Berkley had pulled his whole body into when he'd been preparing to jump on Clover. Anwar didn't look coiled or ready to strike, at all. He was making these pitiful sounds, like he couldn't even draw enough breath to sob properly.

Berkley saw the new cat creeping across the floor towards Anwar, and he ran across the room, reaching the sofa first.

"No," he told Clover. "You don't do this. This is mine. You're not even a real cat. Go AWAY!"

Berkley climbed up on the sofa without even waiting to see if the new cat went away. He rubbed his forehead against Anwar's hand, holding his knee, and licked the web between his fingers a little bit. Anwar let his knees down and made a lap for Berkley. Anwar's hand felt good on his neck, and he let out a deep satisfied purr. But then he heard Anwar say something, in a deep, mournful voice. He sounded hopeless. Berkley looked up at him, and struggled with his urges.

Then Berkley looked over at the new cat, who was watching the whole thing from on top of the bookcase. Berkley narrowed his eyes and told her, "I want to hurt you. But I want to bring back the other human more. If I help you, can you bring the humans back together? Yes or no?"

Clover looked down at him and said, "I think so. I'll do what I can."

A few hours later, Anwar had stumbled out of the house and the cats were alone again. "I keep forgetting who I am," Clover said. "It's hard to hold on to. But I remember, I begged the teachers to help me save you from my family, and I talked about how you were suffering. They said if I understood cats so much, why didn't I try being one? I was like, 'Fine.' I didn't realize what I had signed up for until years later."

"So you climbed into a place that you cannot get

out of again," Berkley suggested. "Because there is not enough room to turn around."

"Sort of, yeah."

"So," said Berkley, tail curled and ears pointed. "Don't turn around."

Anwar's ankle was kind of swollen and he had no money for a doctor visit, and the stain on the bathroom wall had gotten bigger. The Olde Tyme Pub had gotten a totally bullshit citation from the North Carolina Department of Alcohol Law Enforcement, which had the hilarious acronym of ALE. His truck still kept not starting. Anwar longed to rest his head on Joe's shoulder, breathing in that reassuring scent, so Joe could say, *Fuck 'em, it'll all be good.* On his lonesome, Anwar only knew how to spiral.

Clover came up to him as he sat on the bed, getting laboriously dressed, and perched on the edge. She made noises that usually meant "feed me" or "throw my fuzzy ball." Anwar just shrugged, because he'd wasted three days trying to get her to talk.

Just as Anwar finally got his good shirt buttoned and stood up, Clover said, "Hey."

"Well," Anwar said. "Hey."

"Oh thank god. I finally did it. I'm back," Clover

said. "Oh thank goodness. I need your help. I think this is a test, and I'm failing it. One time before, I became a bird, but I needed help to turn back into a person. And now I feel totally stuck in cat form."

Anwar was already reaching for his phone to go on Meeyu and @ that guy, to let him know the cat finally started talking again. He no longer cared if he was being a crazy person. What had sanity done for him lately?

"The longer I go without turning back into a person, the harder it's going to be," Clover said, jumping on the bed. "You look like shit, by the way. Berkley is worried about you. We both are."

"Hey, it's fine. You're okay." Anwar picked her up and looked into her twitchy little face. "I already told those guys, the ones who dropped you off here. They know you're talking again. They're probably on their way. They'll help you out, and maybe they'll give Joe and me some more luck."

Clover squirmed, partly involuntarily. "You really shouldn't take any luck from those guys. It'll come with huge strings attached."

"Well, they told me that you're a liar. And you know, I have nothing to lose." But Anwar had a sudden memory of the man saying, *You wouldn't really be you any more.*

"Please! You have to help me change back to a person before they get here," Clover said.

"I don't know how to do that."

And anyway, it was too late. The door opened, without a knock or Anwar having to unlock it, and a man entered. He had dark skin pitted with acne scars, and long braids, and a purple turtleneck and matching corduroys. "So," the man said, "what does she have to say for herself?"

"You wasted a trip," Clover told him. "I'm still working on changing myself back. I only just got my human voice working. I've got a ways to go before I'm in my own body again."

The man shrugged and picked Clover up with one hand. "You already did what we needed you to do. Just think what we'll be able to do with a cat who talks like a person and knows how to do magic. You'll be way more useful to us in this form." Clover started squirming and shouting, and tried to claw the man, but he had her in a tight grip. He turned to Anwar. "Thanks for whatever you did. We'll consider this a down payment, if you decide you want more luck."

"No!" Clover sounded terrified, on an existential level. "This is messed up. I don't want to be stuck as a cat forever. I have a boyfriend. I have friends. You have to help me!" She looked right at Anwar, her yellow eyes fixed on him, and said, "You can't let them take me."

Anwar thought about how things had been before, with just the one cat, and Joe there, and everything peaceful. He wanted nothing more than to bring back that version of his life. But he looked at Clover, her whole body contorted with terror—claws out, eyes huge and round, mouth full of teeth. And he knew what Joe would say if he was here: *You gotta live like the fuckers don't own you.*

The words came out before Anwar had even thought them through: "You can't take my cat."

"I beg your pardon?" the man said. His stare was impossible to meet.

"You can't," Anwar swallowed. "That's my cat. You can't take her."

"Thank you thank you," Clover whispered.

"This isn't a cat. She's a whole other thing. And whatever she told you, she was lying. That's what she does."

Anwar drew courage from the fact that the weird man was arguing with him, instead of just taking the cat and leaving. "You gave this cat to me. You didn't say it was a loan. She's mine. I have all the records to prove it."

And now the man did turn to leave, but Clover leapt out of his arms. She landed on three feet, nearly tumbled head over tail, and then got her balance fast enough to run back into the apartment. She headed for one of the hundred hiding places that she'd gotten to know, but the man was right behind her. Anwar just stood and watched as the man ran through the apartment, knocking over Joe's guitar. He was right on top of Clover, leaning to scoop her up.

There was another cat between the man and Clover. As he bent down to grab the cat who was still shouting in English, his hand connected instead with Berkley. Who bit his thumb, hard enough to draw blood.

Berkley growled at the man, in a pose Anwar had never seen before. Standing his ground, snarling, bloody teeth bared. Roaring. Like a tiny lion. This would have been the most ridiculous sight ever, if it weren't so heroic.

Clover stopped and looked at Berkley, defending her. Her jaw dropped open, her ears were all the way up. "Berkley, shit," she said. "You just bit the thumb of the most powerful man on Earth. I can't believe you. Whatever happens now, I want you to know I regret leaving you behind. And no matter what price I end up paying, I'm glad I rescued you. I'm sorry, and I understand what you went through."

That last phrase was like a string breaking, or a knot being undone after hours of pulling and worrying. As soon as Clover said *understand,* the cat was gone. A naked woman stood in Anwar's hallway, holding Berkley in her arms. He looked up at her and seemed to recognize her. He put his head on her shoulder and purred.

The woman looked at the man, who was nursing his thumb. "I know you're still pissed about Siberia. I get it. But jeez. This was mean, even for you."

The man rolled his eyes, then turned to look at Anwar. "I hope you enjoy not having any luck ever again." Then he stomped out of the apartment, leaving the door open.

As soon as the man was gone, Anwar fell onto the couch, hands on his face. He felt weird having a naked stranger in his home, and even weirder that this girl had seen so much of him at his worst, and he'd had his hand on her face so many times. The whole thing was weird. And he felt a huge letdown in his gut, because he'd convinced himself somehow that he and Joe would get more luck and it would be fine.

"So that's it," Anwar muttered, mostly to himself. "We're screwed."

"Hey, can I borrow some clothes?"

While the girl—Clover—was getting dressed, she tried to talk him down. "Joe is coming back. He loves you, he just sucks at expressing it sometimes. I've seen how you guys are." Somehow, she managed to put clothes on without letting go of Berkley. "So listen. I suck at giving advice. But the absence of good luck is not bad luck. It's just . . . life."

"I guess that sort of makes sense," Anwar said.

"That would be a first for me." Clover looked twitchy, like she was still ready to chase a ball around, or eat a treat out of Anwar's hand. Anwar wondered if she was going to be stuck having cat thoughts forever. "I can fix your injured ankle, no problem. And also I think I know how to get rid of that stain on your bathroom wall. I'll have a look at the truck, I'm pretty good with engines. And I'll leave you my Meeyu info, if you ever have another problem you need help with. I'll be around if you need me, okay?"

Anwar nodded. He was starting to think having this magical girl on speed dial could be better than good luck anyway.

Joe came home an hour later, after Clover had already left. "Hey," Joe said. "I lost my job. But I think we're better off, and I already have a line on something—I'll never have to leave town again. I just wanted to say I'm really sorry about being a jackass, and leaving for so long, and I love you. You're the most beautiful thing I've ever seen."

Anwar just stared at his husband for a moment. He had a case of highway sunburn on one arm and part of his neck, and his hair was a mess, and he looked like a rock star. Anwar threw his arms around Joe and whispered, "The cats missed you." Then he realized there was only cat, and he was going to have to explain somehow. But he was too busy kissing the man he loved, and there would be time for that later.

Watching the two men from the top of his fuzzy climbing tree, Berkley looked immensely self-satisfied.

acknowledgments

The stories in this book were all edited for *Tor.com* by Patrick Nielsen Hayden, whose insightful suggestions, brilliant tangents, and willingness to look at a wide range of ill-advised experiments emboldened me to climb way further onto various limbs. My agent, Russ Galen, has been a constant source of encouragement, feedback, and sage career advice, and meanwhile Nate Miller with Manage-Ment has been a wise and steadfast advocate as various people asked about the film and TV rights for "Six Months, Three Days." I'm also supremely grateful to Eric Garcia, Krysten Ritter, Lindsey Liberatore, David Janollari, and everyone else involved with the effort to turn "Six Months" into a TV show. Meanwhile, I'm grateful to the many other editors whose help and encouragement improved my efforts at short fiction, including Jed Hartman, Karen Meisner, Susan Groppi, John Joseph Adams, Peter Rubin, Charles

Coleman Finlay, Sheila Williams, Jonathan Strahan, Christie Yant, Navah Wolfe, Dominik Parisien, Ed Finn, Kathryn Cramer, Kelly Link, Gavin Grant, Heather Shaw, Howard Junker, Nick Mamatas, Michelle Tea, Clint Catalyst, Lance Cleland, Eric Spitznagel, Gravity Goldberg, Rudy Rucker, Eileen Gunn, Lynne M. Thomas, Rusty Morrison, John Warner, Elizabeth McKenzie, Carol Queen, Daphne Gottlieb, Stephen Elliott, and countless others. I also have to thank the many, many people who have given me feedback on these stories and others, including Claire Light, Liz Henry, Nabil, Saladin Ahmed, Na'amen Tilahun, d.g.k. goldberg, the Revisionaries of Raleigh, and others far too numerous to single out. Finally, my life partner and coconspirator, Annalee Newitz, was willing to listen to my oddball story ideas at all hours of the day—while also sharing her own luminous speculations and genius story ideas with me.

about the author

Charlie Jane Anders's 2016 novel *All the Birds in the Sky* was a national bestseller. Earlier, her debut novel *Choir Boy* (2005) won a Lambda Literary Award. Her journalism and other writing has appeared in, among other venues, *Salon, Mother Jones,* and *The Wall Street Journal*. She was for many years the managing editor of the website *io9*. She lives in the San Francisco Bay area.